Jack of Hearts

HONEYBEE HOLLOW

ARIELLA TALIX

Cover Design by Dar Albert, Wicked Smart Designs

E-book ISBN: 979-8-9895156-5-3

Paperback ISBN: 979-8-9895156-6-0

One

Jack

"Jack, you need to stop doing this to yourself," Dr. Alister tells me. "You've been in therapy with me for six months, and you've professed to be in love four times, each time with a different person. It's great, in a way, that you're so open to people, and obviously you have a lot of love to give, but you're setting yourself up for a lot of heartache. Maybe you need to take a break from dating and focus on friendships for a while. You're not giving your affection to worthy candidates, and I hate to see your heart getting trampled over and over."

"Yeah, Doc, I know. But Melissa was so pretty and seemed so sweet…"

"Until she stole your car and crashed it."

"Well, true. But I got it back eventually, and the dent wasn't too bad."

"And what about the disappearing yoga instructor? He just about crushed you."

"I know. But those muscles… and he was all bendy. He made me drool."

"Jack, physical attraction is not love. You're equating sex with something deeper, and that isn't necessarily true."

"I know. It hurt like the dickens when he skipped town after using me like his favorite plaything. I was sure he'd just gone out to get us coffee. I told him I loved him, fell asleep, and woke up to find him gone!"

"And how many times did you text him before he blocked you?"

"Uh… seven? Eight? Something like that."

"And before he left for 'coffee,' how much did he swipe from your wallet?"

I sigh, "Yeah… all my cash, but at least he didn't take my credit cards or my license. And besides, it wasn't just me he did this to. The yoga studio closed, and no one's heard from him in months. The building owner is pretty pissed off."

"He's probably been stealing from a lot of folks and had to get out of town. At least he most likely didn't target you specifically. But, Jack, do you enjoy being crushed?"

"Not at all. I swear, I'm not *trying* to get my heart broken.

That's the last thing I want. I get so caught up in the good stuff, I guess I forget to look for red flags."

Our conversation goes along like this for a while, and I truly do get it. Dr. Alister is cool. He confided in me that he's also bisexual which attracted me to him right off the bat. I must admit I have a crush on him, although we have only "met" via video chats. I guess he lives up in Indiana somewhere. I'm pretty sure he's in a committed relationship from the details he's let slip, but… a guy can dream. I started counseling with him when my cousin recommended I find someone to chat with. She recognized what she called my "love addiction" and thought I needed help. Anyway, she has a friend who swears by his advice.

I live in a small town in eastern Kentucky called Honeybee Hollow. Back in the day, the town used to be pretty depressed, but a bright young mayor—Tanner Lassiter—was voted into office. He did wonders—encouraged economic growth, drew artists and restaurant owners from all over the state. His hard work put the town on the map.

Lassiter went on to become the governor of Kentucky (the youngest in state history!), and he recently retired from politics. I guess he'd done what he set out to do and prefers a quiet, private life with his family now. I don't know if it's true or not, but there are whispered rumors he has a polyamorous marriage. He's a great guy and deserves all the happiness he can find. So, if he does have a wife *and* husband, I can see why he'd get out of politics and the fishbowl he was scrutinized in. I wish them all the best.

Since Lassiter's time, Honeybee Hollow has flourished into a vacation destination and a haven for the arts, and I was drawn to it. I run a lovely eclectic gallery and live in the apartment above it.

The gallery has two main areas—the front is reserved for local Kentucky artists, and I sell pieces in a wide price range there. The rear room is for special curated shows I rotate every four to six weeks, so keeping up with all of that is a lot of work. The rest of the gallery space is storage and a private work room.

The problem with Honeybee Hollow is that the population is tiny—fewer than 3,000 residents, and it's a place people come to for all kinds of romantic things like *getting married.* I'm not exactly in the best spot for finding true love for myself, even though that's my main goal in life. I can't help it —I'm a romantic.

I love it here in Honeybee Hollow. The air is fresh, and the surrounding mountains are picturesque. People come here to hike and enjoy the beautiful scenery, plus we have a huge number of bed and breakfasts where couples come to relax. I drove down here with my girlfriend a while back and loved the atmosphere, so I sold my house in Lexington and relocated. She was going to move here with me, but she ghosted me, and that seriously bummed me out for a while. I thought we had something extra special, but I eventually made myself move on. I've been trying a bit too hard to fill the hole she left in my heart because I've made some poor decisions about people since then.

Anyway, I bought this building and renovated it to accommodate a gallery downstairs and my living quarters upstairs. It's a great commute! Also, it's a change for me not having a household staff, but for now I'm enjoying a simple life in a smaller place I can manage by myself. I'll build another house sometime… maybe. But for now, I'm living an uncomplicated life.

Even though Honeybee Hollow has a small population, I find myself convinced I'm falling in love repeatedly. Something needs to happen, and it's time to make a change.

$$\heartsuit\heartsuit\heartsuit$$

I THINK I HAVE JUST THE TICKET, THANKS TO DR. ALISTER'S stellar advice.

I'm going to have a party. Not a champagne, cheese, and crackers gallery opening kind of party—maybe a smaller group for… oh… poker night! I'll have it up here in my apartment instead of downstairs around the art. This will be completely out of character for me. I have room to seat maybe eight people, and I'll make my dining room table into a game table. I need to figure out my guest list. I know enough of the locals now to fill up the place. And there are a few of them I'd definitely like to get to know better.

I send out a text message to ten people since I'm sure not everyone can make it.

> Jack Hartz: Hi! Can you come to my apartment this Saturday at 8 p.m. for a night of penny ante poker? You probably know, but just as a reminder, I live above the gallery Imagine on Third St. Bring your best poker face and plenty of change, and I'll provide the cards, refreshments, and fun!

Four people send their regrets that they already have plans or they're horribly sick with a flu bug. One of the messages bounced, so apparently I was given a bad number, but two people respond favorably.

> Juniper Barry: Thanks, Jack. That sounds like a fun first date! See you Saturday.

First date? Did I give off that kind of vibe? Huh. I read back over our messages and decide Juni Barry is more than anxious to get to know me. Now I'm getting excited about seeing her. She's really cute and just recently moved here. She opened Hot Stuff—the new coffee house on Main Street. Why didn't she notice it was a group message, though? Maybe she was in a hurry; she's always busy. Anyway, I'm stoked she's coming.

Jack Hartz: Great, Juni. Looking
forward to Saturday.

The next reply is from the guy who manages the nearby campground. He's a real outdoorsy type and looks amazing in hiking shorts. I met him not too long ago at a picnic.

Asher Bellamy: Sounds good. I'll be
there. Thanks! I look forward to
seeing you.

Jack Hartz: Great! See you Saturday.

So, that leaves three prospective guests I have yet to hear from. They still have plenty of time to let me know.

I try to think of a few more people I could maybe invite. There's the friendly guy from the grocery store, but he tends to have terrible BO, so I quickly discount him. We'll be sitting too close at the table if he doesn't take a shower and put on a clean shirt. I go through all of the non-tourists who've visited the gallery recently and come up with a bunch of married or coupled-up people. I guess I could invite some of them, but it doesn't sound like as much fun as other singles. I know, I know… I'm not supposed to be trolling for dates—just looking for friends. So, I send the same text to a nice couple I met at the picnic where I met Asher, but I hear back that they've split up and are both moving out of town this weekend. Ouch.

A couple of days later, I get a response from the woman who cuts my hair. She has the best sense of humor, so I was excited to see her away from her shop, but she sends her regrets, saying she has a terrible cough or cold and doesn't want to spread it around. She may have already spread it, though, because the other two replies I have say nearly the same thing. Sore throats and bad coughs. Yuck. It sounds as if half the town has this bug. I'm glad they're all staying home and keeping their germs to themselves. People seem a lot more responsible about that than they used to be—maybe one good thing came out of the pandemic.

So, it's going to be the three of us, I guess. At least Juni and Asher are fun people. I wonder if they know each other. Well, we'll see!

Two

JUNIPER

I CAN'T WAIT FOR SATURDAY NIGHT! MOVING TO HONEYBEE Hollow right at the foot of the mountains was a dream of mine ever since I heard about the town, and now I have a new friend and an evening to anticipate. Jack Hartz is such a cutie-pie in an apple-cheeked, messy blond kind of way. He's tall and hunky and has a boyish face and wide-eyed expression that would make you mistake him for sixteen years old if it weren't for his deep voice and that ripped body of his.

He mentioned he likes yoga and hiking, so he stays fit, that's for sure. He likes to come into Hot Stuff early before opening his gallery and always orders a large black coffee, so he's not into any of the frou-frou sweet drinks. You can tell a few things about someone by what they order and how they treat their barista. Jack is as polite as they come and always tips generously. I've had a crush on him since he first walked through the door. His smile just knocks me out.

I've always kinda wondered, though, if he's gay. What a bummer that would be! For me anyway, not for him. He'd no doubt be fine with whatever he is. But he asked me out, so I guess he's not. Yay!

Ohmygosh! I just checked his text again and I'm so freakin' embarrassed! I assumed he was asking me out on a date, but now I realize he's also invited a whole bunch of other people to his place. He didn't correct me, so maybe he wants me to be his date anyway. I suppose I'll get to meet other people too. Maybe some of them haven't been into Hot Stuff yet, so I don't know them. Sales have been slow the past few days because there's a flu bug going around, but maybe if I meet some new folks, it will be good for business.

Would Jack think it's dumb if I brought him one of our Hot Stuff shirts to wear? One of the blue ones would bring out the color of his eyes, and people would definitely take a second look on that bod of his. Eh, maybe that would be too much. I don't want him to think he has to advertise my business.

I'll at least take some of the cranberry oatmeal cookies he seemed to like. The one time I offered him a treat on the house, that was what he asked for anyway. He probably thought it was the healthiest choice. I ought to bring some chocolate chip ones too for the real cookie fans. Maybe we can all munch on them while we play poker.

And speaking of that, I need to Google poker rules, so I don't make a fool of myself! I know aces are high, and I know the suits, but flushes and straights? I've heard the terms, but I don't have a clue what they mean.

And what is a wild card? I have to do my homework. People have always told me they can read my thoughts on my face, so I'm going to have to practice my poker face in the mirror tonight. I don't want to lose too badly. Maybe I can just watch Jack and learn from what he does. He's certainly no hardship to look at.

Now… what should I wear? Maybe something that shows lots of cleavage and distracts people? The weather is pretty hot, so I can get away with a skimpy top and a pair of shorts or skinny jeans. Or maybe a short skirt… hmm… I should show off my legs for sure. Maybe I'll hit a boutique or two for a new outfit after I close Hot Stuff for the day. I'm open from seven a.m. to three p.m., and the shops will be open until six. I've always been a morning person, so this suits me just fine. Sundays and Mondays are my days off, so I can stay up late on Saturday and play poker if I take a nap that afternoon.

This is going to be great!

Three

Asher

Well, well, well! The cute artsy guy must be a little more interested than I finally decided he was. I thought we hit it off really well at the picnic when I met him, but after I gave him my number, it was crickets for a few weeks. Maybe he's shy and took a while to contact me. Or maybe he's into someone else and just feels like having a party. In any case, I won't mind seeing more of him. And by more of him, I mean *all* of him. Sure, I could have texted him myself, but I wasn't too clear about how he rolls, so I left it up to him. I was pretty certain I was getting the vibe from him, but he was also flirting with a couple of the ladies.

I shouldn't complain. I probably confuse people too.

That's what being bi does for you. I'm an equal opportunity lover, and by that, I mean I love it all.

I love poker too, and I'm damn good at it. I'm so glad I'll have a night off this weekend and can play. We have a rare break between corporate retreat sessions at the camp. Summertime is usually jam-packed, but due to the schedules of two large groups, we have a built-in hiatus. Couldn't come at a better time. Although I enjoy my job, I've been suffering a little summer burnout from the repetitive nature hikes and the forced cheerfulness while leading businesspeople in trust games day in and day out. I'd love to tip back some drinks and relax with normal adult conversation. My God, that sounds so good.

I shouldn't go over empty-handed, though. I should stop and pick something up before I head over.

Looking around at the choices, I text Jack:

Asher Bellamy: Hey Jack. I'm at the liquor store on my way over to your place. What's your poison? They have a killer tequila—or are you more of a bourbon kind of guy? Beer preference?

> Jack Hartz: Wow, thanks, Asher. You don't have to bring anything. I have plenty of beer and soft drinks, and we have a smaller group than expected because of the flu going around. I am pretty fond of tequila, but it's up to you. See you soon. ;) Oh—I even have a few limes.

Tequila it is then. Does he have shot glasses? I pick up a bottle of the good stuff and a box of six glasses. Now I'm ready to party! Am I supposed to be his date? Maybe I should have asked. After all, he did send me a wink with his text. I guess I'll just assume it's a date until someone tells me otherwise.

Jack's apartment is surprisingly large for something over a retail space. It's all beautiful hardwood floors, comfy colorful furniture, and large windows designed to allow people to take in the view. Honeybee Hollow is nothing if not picturesque, and I love living here. It's going on sunset time, so the view of the mountains and the town is spectacular.

When the job at the camp became available, I snapped it up as fast as I could, and I've been happy there. My previous career goal fizzled when I discovered I wasn't suited to it at all. Just one more thing my family probably would have griped at me about if they'd cared. At least I figured it out before wasting half my life being miserable and taking it out on the people around me. And it's not like I took money from my parents to get my education. They made it clear I was paying my own way, and that suited me just fine.

Anyway, Honeybee Hollow's a great little community, and I'm happy here.

As I saunter into his place, I notice Jack taking a good, long look at me from top to bottom, so I give him a wink. "Here ya go, buddy," I say as I hand him the tequila and shot glasses. "Nice place." I'm tempted to give him a quick kiss, but he's a little shy. Better get the lay of the land before I do any lip locking, I guess.

"Thanks, Asher." Jack says. "You really didn't need to, but I love this brand." He turns slightly and adds, "I want you to meet my friend Juniper Barry. Have you been to her coffee house Hot Stuff yet? It's over on Main Street, and she's doing a great job. She also brought us some of her delicious cookies." He reaches for her hand and brings her closer before dropping it. "Juni, this is Asher Bellamy who runs the campground outside of town."

"I'm delighted to meet you, Juni," I say as sincerely as I can because… wow. This lady is a knockout. She has legs for miles, and she is not shy about showing off in her mini skirt. And her golden waves cascade around her shoulders, highlighting some dangerous cleavage I could get lost in. I clasp her hand, wishing it were her waist instead. I suddenly want to kiss the daylights out of those full lips of hers. But then she goes and opens her mouth, and I'm a goner.

"It's nice to meet you too, Asher," she says in a low, almost gravelly voice I swear vibrates through me and wrings me out. "Bellamy… 'beautiful friend.' Such a wonderful name. And your first name means 'gift from God.' But you probably knew all of that and think I'm silly."

"Too bad my parents didn't keep thinking that after they got to know me better." Juni and Jack don't know what to make of that statement, so I quickly add, "I'd never think anything about you was silly." I turn to Jack. "Isn't she just about the most captivating woman you've ever seen?"

"Oh stop," she says with a throaty chuckle. Even her laugh is sexy, and I need to hear more of it.

"He's right," Jack tells us both. "Juni, you are the loveliest woman I know."

"Well, thank you. I'm probably hopeless at poker, though, so bear with me tonight, you two. I'm a complete newbie." And there goes that throaty laugh again. Good lord.

"Is this it for your guest list?" I ask Jack as I glance around and see no one else.

He nods. "I tried for a full house—that's poker humor," he says to Juni with a little grin. "But too many people are staying home because they're sick this week. I'm frankly glad they're all responsible about that." He looks at both of us and continues, "I'm happy you both could come, though. Let's get comfortable and play, alright? We can draw, and high card is dealer, then we can rotate around. If you want to change the game, it's dealer's choice."

"Any more rules?" I ask.

"Hmm, nope. Not unless the dealer makes some up."

Juni looks confused, so I suggest, "Jack, why don't you just do the honors and deal. It sounds like Juni might need a few pointers."

I head to the kitchen sink like I own the place, rinse out the new shot glasses, pick up the bowl of sliced lime wedges Jack prepared, and then we arrange ourselves around his table. We make piles of our change in front of us, and I pour us all a shot of tequila.

Jack tears the plastic wrapper off a brand-new deck, removes the jokers, and shuffles, saying, "Five card draw. Nothing is wild. Keeping it simple." He tells us, "Ante up," and we toss pennies onto the middle of the table. He deals us each five cards, and Juni's face breaks into a grin. I have to stifle a laugh. The woman does *not* have a poker face.

Jack looks at me, so I toss in a nickel and say, "Five cents." I look at Juni and ask, "Do you see or raise the bet?"

"Um…"

"'See' means you match my bet, 'raise' means you think you have better cards, so you want to pay more into the pot and try to get us to match it, and 'fold' means you think you'll lose if you stay in this hand, and you don't want to waste your money."

"I raise you a nickel," she says and tosses in a dime.

"Wow. Heavy stakes already," Jack says with a laugh. "I see your ten cents." He looks at me, and I lay down one card. He deals me a new one and turns to Juni. "How many cards do you want?"

"Do I have to give up any if I don't want to?" she asks, and I try not to laugh again.

"No, you can do whatever you want with your hand," Jack answers politely. When she smiles at him and holds her cards close to her chest shaking her head, he says, "Dealer takes four," and he deals to himself and it's my turn again.

"I bet ten cents." I toss in a dime. "Juni, are you still going to raise me?"

"I'm putting in a quarter," she says with great confidence.

"Phew. That's too rich for my blood. Dealer folds. Asher? You still in?" Jack tosses his cards down, and I come up with fifteen cents to meet Juni's raise.

"I call," I tell Juni. "Let's see what you have, beautiful."

"Can't I raise you again?" she asks hopefully.

"'Fraid not." She's either completely clueless or a great faker.

"Okay then." Juni's grin is wide as she lays down a full house—two sevens and three queens.

"Well, well," I say as I lay down my pair of tens and slowly lay down one ace, a second ace, and then pause dramatically until I lay down a stupid four. "So close. Congratulations. Full house beats two pair, even when it's aces high."

We all toss back our shots of tequila. Juni shudders and blinks and scoops up her winnings from her full house. "This is fun," she says chuckling, and then proceeds to lose the next several hands to either Jack or me. We laugh a lot and practice our poker chatter, ribbing each other. Jack goes on a winning streak for a while, then Juni wins a few more until my luck changes dramatically and I start to clean them both out. I even manage to draw to an inside royal flush and surprise myself. That one prompted another round of celebratory tequila shots.

The stacks of change grow and grow in front of me, but Jack is nearly tapped out. He loses one more time, and when it's his turn to ante up, he whips off his shirt and tosses it into the pot. I grin at his chest as Juni gasps, "Jack!"

"What? I still might win, and I'm out of change. If I win this hand, I'll put it back on."

I pour Jack another shot. "I wouldn't want our host to feel chilly. This oughtta keep you warmed up."

But when I go to pour another for Juni, she puts her hand over her glass and says, "Thanks Asher, but I think I'll switch to soft drinks now." She takes a bite of a cookie, amused, and sashays over to the refrigerator where she selects a bottle of soda.

Apparently, she's as comfortable in Jack's place as I am for whatever reason. And Jack seems fine with us both rummaging around in his kitchen.

After losing that hand to me as well—which included his shirt and belt—Jack gets up and closes his drapes. He winks at me when he comes back toward the table, clearly noticing my scrutiny of his toned abs and pecs. He tells us, "Once it's dark out, this place is a little like living in a fishbowl. I'm glad you got to enjoy the sunset though. Would anyone else like to take a break and have a snack?" He pulls a platter out of the refrigerator with cut up fruit, cheese, and pieces of deli meat. It's an attractive charcuterie board. Then he produces some chips and guacamole.

"Did you get the food ready for the party before all the others said they couldn't come?" I ask.

Jack blushes a little. "Actually, no. I just didn't know what the two of you would like, and I thought I'd offer a variety. I also have pretzels and popcorn." He gives me another wink. Surely this is his brand of flirting, but he's also done it to Juni, I've noticed.

"The perfect host," Juni says, dipping a chip into the guac. "Mmm, Jack, this is delicious!" She's eyeballing his torso and likes what she sees. Suddenly I want her eyes on me the same way, so I'm going to have to do something about that.

Four

Physically, these guys are too much. Jack looks like he grew up surfing—though that's implausible in Kentucky, but he also has an intelligent, soft side to him. What originally got him interested in art? I keep forgetting to ask because I get caught up in whatever he's talking about. He has several beautiful pieces around his apartment, and when he showed me around his gallery a few weeks ago, it was filled with fantastic work. He has a terrific sense of style and artistry although he claims he's no artist himself. I remember being distracted while he gave me the tour, though, because I kept wishing he'd kiss me. I have it bad for the guy, that's for sure.

Asher, on the other hand, was born for the outdoors. He's

too big to be contained inside; I'm guessing he's around six foot five. I wonder if he's ever played football or some other very physical sport. He looks like someone who could crush a brick barehanded but would hold a kitten in his palm like it was a precious gem. He's covered with colorful tattoos and could use a haircut, but his black hair shines like obsidian. What sort of heritage gives a man such beautiful coloring and hair so thick and dark? His eyes are a golden brown like cognac, and the skin around his tattoos is deeply suntanned. He's as stunning as Jack in a completely different way, and he's obviously super smart. I want to rub up against him like a cat in the worst way.

I get the feeling from both men that I could trust them with my life, and that makes me warm inside. This warmth has nothing to do with the tequila.

While we sit and snack, we get into a lengthy conversation about our lives and careers, and the time flies by. I'm impressed they both have advanced degrees. Jack earned an MBA after studying art history at the University of Kentucky, and Asher studied plant biology up at Purdue and then got a PhD. He was planning to be a botany professor until he decided he didn't like being indoors teaching all the time. No surprise there.

I share with them how I grew up working in my parents' all-organic health food restaurant in Berea doing a little of everything and then took courses in baking and business while I worked as a barista through college. I always wanted to have my own café, and while I honored my hippie parents' commitment to their principles, I wanted to appeal to a larger audience beyond the crunchy community.

When the opportunity to open Hot Stuff in Honeybee Hollow came up, I couldn't resist. I poured every last dollar I had into the business along with some hefty loans. I'm having a lot of fun with it, even though it's exhausting work, and I desperately need a couple more employees. I'll get there. Like Jack, I have an upstairs apartment, only I find it a little cramped and too close to the business sometimes, but I'll have to live with smelling like coffee until I can move.

It's nice getting to know them like this. It feels as if we've been friends for years, we all get along so well. My inhibitions are loosened up, and I find myself blurting out, "So, Jack… when you invited me over, I thought you were asking me on a date. I'm sorry if I made you uncomfortable about that."

There's a moment of awkward silence, during which Asher's eyes dart between Jack and me. Jack's a little stunned, and his mouth hangs open as his brain tries to catch up.

Before Jack can respond, Asher offers, "I wondered the same thing. I thought I might be your date for the night. Kinda hoped so anyway." He flashes a blinding smile Jack's way as if to say, "No hard feelings."

"Oh, uh…" Jack's face turns red. "Thank you both. Honestly, I'd love to have dates with *both* of you, but I've been counseled to look for friendship for a while. That's why I tried to get a bunch of people to come over. I want to have fun, but not get… um… involved, you know?"

"Who said anything about 'involved'?" Asher asks. "You can date without any deep shit going on, can't you?"

Jack gives a self-deprecating chuckle and answers, "Apparently, I can't. And I have an amazing ability to attract the wrong sorts of people and fall in love with them, over-looking the fact that they're worthless scum."

"Jack!" I say, completely miffed.

"Present company excluded," he says sincerely with both hands raised in surrender. "I know you're both responsible people, and I'd love to get to know both of you better. I just… um… It's probably better if we keep things from getting too sexy."

"Is that why you started taking off your clothes?" Asher asks laughing.

"I was out of coins! But… um… yeah. I kind of like taking them off. I hope I didn't embarrass either of you."

"Not me," Asher says. He's eyeing Jack's body with a lot of interest.

"Not in the least. I love the view," I tell him and give him the once-over as well. I still want to understand the whole picture though, so I ask, "Jack, I'm sort of catching on that you're bi. Is that right?"

"Yes."

"Hot damn!" Asher crows and rubs his hands together. "Anyone else up for a threesome?"

Five

OH BOY, NOW I'VE DONE IT. WHY DID I TAKE OFF MY SHIRT and open *this* can of worms? Dr. Alister would be so disappointed in me. My heart is suddenly pounding, and I see nothing but lust in Asher's beautiful whiskey-colored eyes, and Juni's nodding and looks like she's won the billion-dollar lottery. I need to pull my thoughts together, so I get to my feet and announce, "Excuse me, I need to hit the bathroom for a minute."

Not only is Asher suggesting something I've wanted for years, he's serious, and Juni's obviously more than amenable. I scoot into my bedroom and close the door. I have to compose myself for a moment and take a few deep breaths.

Dr. Alister has a special phone number he gives his clients that he stresses is for emergencies *only*, and anyone who abuses it will be blocked. But without a second thought, I dial it. It rings a few times, and I'm about to give up because I suddenly realize it's awfully late to be calling him. Before I disconnect, however, he answers—sounding wide awake at least.

"Jack. What's going on?" I hear the concern in his voice. "Are you alright?"

"Uh, sorry to bother you so late. I just needed to talk to you." My words tumble out so fast, it's a wonder he can understand me. "I asked some people to come over tonight to play cards, and I'm trying to be *friends* the way you and I discussed, but they seem to be up for a *threesome*. What do I do?" I hate how my voice went all squeaky when I said "threesome." Way to play it cool. I gulp in air.

Dr. Alister actually chuckles. He *laughs*! "How do you feel about that, Jack? Do you have a moral problem with it, or does the idea embarrass you? Is this two men, two ladies?"

"One of each," I clarify. "And no, I don't have any moral problem with it. It sounds amazing. But will I get hurt again?"

"What kind of people are they?"

"They're *good* people. Smart. Professional. Beautiful… and um… nice. So nice."

"I want you to think hard about this question and answer honestly. Do you see *any* red flags?"

Pausing a moment to think back over our conversation

tonight, I answer finally, "No. None. They are good, honest, hard-working people, and they're as sexy as fu… hell."

"Jack, I'm going to share something with you, but first I also need to tell you I'm… ah… taking a new job soon, and I'm going to have to refer you to a colleague of mine for any future counseling. I'm sorry to break this to you right now, but in the light of what I'm going to say, it's important." He hesitates a second. "I… ah… have been in a serious relationship with a man *and* a woman for the better part of a year now, and it's the best thing that's ever happened to all three of us. You know I don't normally share much of my personal life, but I want to let you know if it's meant to be, it could be wonderful for you as well. Just be sure these are people whom you can trust. It can get complicated."

"Oh!" I knew he was bi, but I had no idea. This does sort of normalize it all for me. "So I ought to give it a try?"

"Only if you think you can handle it. If these two people are as nice as you say, you might want to go for it. If it all falls apart right away… I'll tell you what. Keep this number, and I'll talk to you if you need me, even after I quit my private practice. I'm here for you, Jack. If this turns out to be a one-time thing, don't beat yourself up about that. There aren't any rules. Remember that. Just tell yourself you were in it for some fun, and don't let yourself get hurt. If it turns out to be more, then I'm happy for you."

"Wow. Thanks. I'm sorry I called so late, and I hope I didn't disturb anything important." He chuckles at me, so I think I did disturb something. "Good night, Dr. Alister. Thank you again."

"Call me Weston, Jack. We're friends. Good luck. I hope for the best for you. Good night."

I disconnect and hit the bathroom for good measure and return to the living room where I find that Asher and Juni have left the table. They're now side by side on my couch. Kissing! Oh my. They're perfect and so beautiful together. He's so dark and colorful, and she seems like spun gold. I don't want to disturb them, so I head toward the table to put some of the leftover snacks away.

"Where are you going?" Asher asks in a gravelly voice that hits me like Cupid's arrow to the heart. His huge hand wraps around my wrist as I pass by him. God, it feels good. It's warm and strong, like he's claiming me with his grasp. I stop dead in my tracks, close my eyes for a moment, and savor the feel of him.

"We were afraid you might not be coming back, Jack. Are you alright?" Juni asks in her own deep, sexy voice. Her beautiful full lips are even pinker and more kissable now that she's been making out with Asher. "Sit down between us," she commands softly and scoots over.

I close my eyes for a second and whisper, "What you've suggested is my biggest fantasy, and I can hardly contain myself around either of you already. The two of you together might just end me."

Asher lets out a deep rumble of a laugh and pulls me

closer to the couch. "We'll take care of you. Don't worry. It turns out Juni and I have both had some three-way experience, so we'll make sure you enjoy yourself." He hesitates and adds, "Unless this isn't something you want."

"No," I reply quickly. "It's a lot to take in, but I'm not… it's not that I don't want it."

I plunk down on the couch when my knees give way, and Asher looks me in the eye, his expression serious. "Who were you talking to before?" he asks. "We could hear you speaking —just not what you were saying."

"I called my therapist." Now my face is flaming, and I can't look at anything except my own knees.

But out of the corner of my eye, I see Asher nod as he says, "Good idea. Are you okay?" Wow, how refreshingly understanding of him. I like him even more now.

"Surprisingly, yes." As I say this, Juni's soft lips caress the side of my neck, and her hand is gently stroking my chest. I can't suppress the shudder that courses through me.

Confronted with the possibilities we have here, I'm suddenly a little overcome and need to slow things down just a tad, so I ask, "Juni, can you tell us about your threesome? What did you do—if you don't mind me asking?"

She smiles understandingly at me and sits back. "I don't mind. It was different from us. I had mine with my college boyfriend and my roommate, actually. So it was two women and one man."

"Oh? And did you enjoy it?" I ask.

"I did enjoy it physically, but we never did it again. In fact, my relationship ended soon after that, and I had no desire to have sex with my roommate. That bummed her out, but… too bad. It was fun for the one time."

"So…" Asher prompts, "what did you guys do? Tell us, Juni. We want to be… titillated."

She clears her throat and chuckles. "We took turns blowing my boyfriend until he asked us to do it together and kiss each other while we were licking him. He seemed to really like it, but he stopped us and asked my roommate to eat my pussy. He said he always wanted to see that up close. He pulled me onto his lap so she could do it. It kind of freaked me out at first, but I tried to relax. And when she started, I immediately appreciated how well a woman can do that for another woman. You know… familiarity with the anatomy and all. She knew how to use her tongue and how to finger fuck me just right. It was pretty amazing. I came really quickly, but she didn't want to quit. She told my boyfriend to fuck me in the butt while she kept playing with me, and they'd get an even bigger orgasm out of me that way."

She pauses for a moment, and I have to ask, "Did they?" My voice sounds raw and hoarse.

"Oh yes. Absolutely." Juni's face is as red as a cardinal. "I've never experienced anything like it."

Asher looks turned on and confused at the same time as he asks, "So why didn't you want to keep playing with your roommate after that if it felt so good?"

She squinches up her face a little and thinks before answering. "I don't know. I guess I never really craved that kind of attention from her after that. She was an okay person, but I certainly felt no affection or attraction. I was just done with the experiment."

"I see," he says.

I think I see as well. "So how did you end the 'session' or whatever you want to call it?" I ask.

"My boyfriend fucked my ass until he came, then he went down on my roommate. He wanted me to do it, but I didn't want to. I was honestly kind of embarrassed by the whole thing. It was sexy, but it downplayed any real affection we might have had for each other. Does that make sense?"

"Yes," we say together. But Asher goes on to say, "If you had stronger feelings for either of them, I guarantee it would have been a much better result for you."

"I can see that. I already feel more strongly for the both of you than I did for either of them, so I'm frankly dying to try it with you," she says. "But, Asher, will you tell us about your experience too?"

Asher grins. "It was during college too. I had a friend who was also bi and who was dating a girl. She found out from him that I was bi, and she pestered him into letting us both have sex with her. She wanted to watch two men together, and she wanted to be the focus of two men's attention on her. Plus… she'd been flirting with me for months whenever he wasn't looking."

"Uh oh," I say. "That sounds like trouble."

Asher nods at me. "It was. But I was up for the experience anyway. Even though I didn't like her much, she was gorgeous, and I was horny—so I didn't have much to lose. I got to enjoy sucking some dick when he and I did some sixty-nine, and then my buddy and I DP'ed her."

"How did things turn out for all of you after that?" I ask.

"I guess she wouldn't shut up about it, and for weeks she kept asking him to set things up with me again. She was never satisfied with just him after that, he told me, so he finally gave up on her. He and I hooked up a few more times until we graduated, and he moved away to go to grad school elsewhere. I have no idea what happened to her. She tried calling me a few times until I blocked her number. She just seemed like a troublemaker. I did enjoy the DP, though. That was amazing." He looks at me seriously and adds, "You haven't lived until you've felt your dick rubbing up against another guy *inside* a woman. It's incredible."

I feel a jerking sensation in my pants and ask in a voice way too squeaky for my taste, "Would the two of you like to play here, or in the bedroom?"

Asher ignores my question and leans in caressing my lips with his. He's gentle for about ten seconds until I relax, then his tongue slides its way into my mouth, and he takes over like he's going to eat me alive. I've never been kissed like this before. I swear something unnamable is burning me from within. I feel cherished, desired, and so *alive*. Why is this so different from all previous kisses?

Juni nibbles my earlobe, and she's playing with my nipple, making me squirm. "Do you like this, Jack?" she whispers in my ear, and her voice makes a thrilling tickle run down my spine. I can feel my dick aching to break loose from the confines of my pants, and I'm awfully uncomfortable down there. The rest of me is silently singing the Hallelujah chorus though.

All I can do by way of an answer is whisper, "Don't stop."

They both laugh softly at my desperation, and the sound rumbles through me, causing my dick to twitch again.

Asher's hand is stroking my thigh, and I can barely stop myself from ordering him to move it up to where he'll do me some real good. The dampness in my boxers tells me I'm leaking pre-cum, I'm so fucking turned on. My heart is beating like a hummingbird right now.

"Kiss Juni," Asher orders me. "She tastes as good as you do." He pulls back and grins at her, telling me, "In fact, I bet she's delicious all over. Wouldn't you love to taste her goodies with me?"

Juni squeezes her legs together and groans a little with that question. She turns her face to mine and leans in to kiss me as Asher asks, "Is this what you meant to have happen when you took off your shirt? Did you want to *play?* Be honest." His hand is still teasing and stroking my thigh. It feels so large and warm and perfect.

I love it.

I stop kissing Juni long enough to answer, "Maybe subconsciously, but I *was* just trying to play cards." I go back to devouring her lips and playing a tongue-battle game. She's amazing. Asher is amazing. My life is suddenly amazing. I'm already falling in love again—only with two people this time. I hope I don't wake up and find out this was a dream.

And I hope it doesn't blow up with twice the usual heartache.

My eyes nearly roll back in my head when I hear my zipper being pulled down. I gather myself and glance down to see Asher doing the honors. Juni's hand leaves my nipple, and she starts unbuttoning her blouse. She pulls away from my mouth long enough to whip her top off, and we're treated to an eyeful of her glorious tits straining at the confines of a lacy bra. Holy knockers that woman has a spectacular body!

"Perfection," Asher whispers, locking eyes on her chest.

Asher grabs the back of his shirt and drags it up and off over his head. He flings it away and grins at us when we both gasp at his body. His tattoos are amazing and beautiful, but even without the graceful body art, his golden skin gleams over his defined muscles. I know I look good, but Asher's body is positively intimidating it's so incredible.

"How do you have time to work?" I ask dumbfounded.

His brow furrows, and he asks, "What are you talking about? I work all the time."

"You must work out all day long to look like this." I wave a hand up and down at his chest and six-pack.

Asher laughs. "Not really. Some of this is genetic, and some is weight training."

"What kind of genetics makes you look like… that?" Juni asks.

Asher laughs again and answers, "My mother is Samoan. Dad's English and Spanish. My guess is her side of the family had more influence in my body type. But I do have to work at making sure all the bulk stays in the right places."

"Whew," she says. "Thank you, Mrs. Bellamy!"

Six

ASHER

I GET THE SENSE FROM JACK THAT HE'S INCREDIBLY TURNED on, but not fully committed to anything too heavy just yet, so I say, "Jack, let's keep things light tonight and go slowly. I don't want anyone getting freaked out because, frankly, I like both of you too much to ruin what we have by letting it get out of hand."

Juni eyes me seriously and says, "You make a lot of sense, Asher. No actual fucking on the first date, okay?"

Jack's entire countenance relaxes, and he exhales. "Thank you, guys. I didn't realize just how nervous I was. You're both amazing, and I want to do everything, but not all at once. Taking it slow sounds, um… slightly painful," he laughs softly, "but wise for now."

I can't help myself, though. His zipper is already down, so I slip my hand inside his pants and give him a little squeeze. He moans and closes his eyes, so I take that as not being too much for him. I stroke up and down his length and admire the feel of him in my hand. He's beautifully endowed, and I need to share this knowledge with Juni. I pull down Jack's boxers, exposing his lovely hard-on, and take Juni's hand to stroke him alongside my hand. "Are you relaxing, Jack?" I ask.

Juni has resumed kissing his neck and nibbling his ear as he groans his affirmative response in a strangled sound.

Jack's dick is absolutely perfect, and it's glistening with pre-cum. I can't stop myself, so I gently remove Juni's hand and lean down into Jack's lap, engulfing his length into my mouth as Juni's fingers curl into the hair on the back of my head. I taste his saltiness and suck him down, hoping for more. He's shaking all over, he's so turned on, and it turns me on so much, I have to stroke myself.

Juni, bless her, sees what I'm doing, and she leaves Jack's ear and slips to her knees in front of me. She unzips me and yanks down my pants and boxers in one giant tug as I lift my hips to accommodate her. Once the pants are down and around one ankle, she shoves my legs apart so she can get close. I get what she's planning—because I'm brilliant that way—and grab a throw pillow for her to kneel on. She smiles, slips it beneath her knees, and grasps my dick with both hands.

Leaning over, she sucks me down the way I've done to Jack. Jack's eyes pop open and he grins at the sight.

"Ohmygod, yes," Jack moans. "I guess we don't need the bed after all. This is so good. So… ohh."

I've tasted plenty of dicks, but somehow Jack's is special. It's hard to describe, but it's as if I need to make love to it with my mouth. I lick him from top to bottom and vary up the pressure of my hand and the patterns I make with my tongue on his sensitive head. He hisses and hums his approval when I make an especially perfect motion, so I'm getting to know his needs. He likes lots of pressure, that's for sure.

Some guys would have already come if I'd given them this kind of attention. Most guys, actually, jizz pretty fast in my mouth. That's what I've come to expect. In fact, for me, giving blowjobs was always a means to an end—getting my partner off was always the goal. But with Jack, it's different. I want to savor him, and I want to convey something through my actions. Just what—I'm afraid to give it a name. I can't be falling for this guy so quickly, can I? I haven't known him long enough.

And Juni… holy cow! She's going to town on me like I'm the finest piece of prime beef she's ever encountered, and I'm about to blow in her mouth. This woman knows her way around a dick, I can tell you! My hips start to rise and fall of their own free will, and it's pretty awkward, given how I'm leaning over Jack's lap at the same time. I just keep thinking, *This is… fun*!

The tension is building in Jack's body, and not surprisingly, he chokes out, "I'm gonna come, Asher!" I squeeze a little harder and increase the suction of my mouth to let him understand my intentions, so he lets loose a stream of cum down my throat with a relieved shout of, "Thank you!"

Well, that's a first. The man has incredibly nice manners for someone having an orgasm. I can't laugh because if I do, I'll choke and probably squirt cum out of my nose, so I just keep swallowing and swallowing and feel myself about to shoot into Juni's mouth, I'm so fucking turned on.

I wave my hand at her and point at my dick, trying to indicate I'm also about to explode. She pops off me and gasps when a flood of jizz goes shooting up into the air and lands all over her chest, narrowly missing her face. She smiles as it hits her, but her eyes widen as Jack reaches over and scoops ejaculate off her and pops his finger into his mouth, sucking it off.

I guess I can say this is one of the sexiest things I've ever done. If this is keeping it low-key, I can't wait for what's next.

Jack stands and grabs some napkins for Juni from the table. He winks at me as he says, "We need to take care of our lady now, Asher. Juni, get comfortable on the couch." He offers her a hand and helps her get situated. I'm still trying to unscramble my brain after that orgasm she just gave me, so I'm kind of slow-witted for a moment—and maybe a little cum-drunk from Jack's explosion in my mouth. Apparently, Jack can multitask better than I can. I scoot over to make room for Juni to get comfortable while I wait for my jumbled brain to rearrange my gray cells into a semblance of order.

Jack's not wasting any time, though. He pushes Juni's barely-there mini skirt up over her hips and grasps the sides of her sexy black lace thong. He makes quick work of sliding it down her legs and pulls it off along with her sandals. They land with a plunk as he tosses them aside, and the lingerie looks so naughty laying atop them. I'm starting to perk up now that my brain has re-energized. It just took one look at the beautiful pussy Jack has revealed for us to enjoy.

Jack slowly begins kissing Juni's thighs and stroking her with both hands. He spreads her legs apart and sits back to admire her. "So beautiful. Look at how wet she is, Asher. Our lovely Juni is so turned on. She needs a kiss."

That sounds like a great idea, so I begin to kiss the daylights out of the woman. As I play with her pretty tits, Jack leans in and tongues her pussy. He makes an appreciative noise and tells me with a groan, "You were right, Asher, her goodies taste wonderful."

Juni shudders as he delves in with his tongue, and I need to watch even more than I need to kiss her, as delightful as kissing her is. I need to see Jack give her this ultimate plea-sure. I am rewarded when he sucks her clit into his mouth, and Juni lets out a protracted moan, "Yessss!"

I shift around so I can maneuver my hand beneath Jack's chin and slide a finger into her soaking warmth. She's tight and slick and shaking with excitement. I slide my finger in and out as Jack licks and sucks until she grasps his head and cries out, "Don't stop!"

Jack chuckles and I reassure her, "Don't worry, sweetheart. We're both too smart to stop."

She's practically squeezing my finger off, but I shove another one in beside it and speed up my actions. Her breathing picks up and she straightens out her legs, going stiff, as she finally falls over the edge in a shuddering climax. Her body seizes up, and she moans something unintelligible. Then spasms of sensation overtake her again and again. She jolts and shakes, and finally her legs relax as she comes back to earth.

Jack gives her one last lick and sits up as I slip my fingers out of her satiny pussy. I suck them clean and announce, "Yep. Delicious."

I'd say for the first time together, we've done an amazing job of pleasing one another. I can't wait to do this… and more… as often as possible. From their blissed-out faces, I think we have a consensus.

I'm just about to suggest we all head into Jack's bedroom for more fun and frolic when Jack stands and asks, "Does anyone else need a drink of water?"

Seven

I'M TRYING NOT TO FREAK OUT RIGHT NOW. THAT WAS amazing. As I hoist up my pants, I'm suddenly parched and in dire need of water. My pulse is still beating in my ears, I swear. Without waiting for either of my guests to answer, I grab three bottles of water out of the refrigerator and hand them out. If all indications are correct, Juni and Asher are as blown away as I am. Their facial expressions make them seem completely overcome, but they also have a look in their eyes that asks, "Was that real?" I mean… what we did wasn't all that unusual or anything, but it seemed so… *exceptional*.

I snag my shirt off the table and start to put it back on, too, when Asher pipes up with a teasing tone and asks, "Hey, what are you doing? I won that shirt fair and square. If you want to get dressed, you'll have to win it back."

I laugh and shrug. I doubt at this point it would bother them to see me half-naked in my own home, so I drop the shirt. They, however, are putting all their clothes back on. I sit back down on the couch between them and ask, "So what do you both think of your first dates with me? Pretty hot? Too much? Needs work?"

They both burst out laughing, and Juni answers, "I'm looking forward to many more dates, Jack, and I hope it can be all three of us. This was… deliciously decadent and positively thrilling."

"Phew!" Asher exclaims. "I'm glad it's not just me. I feel a little odd saying this, but whatever it is that we all have going with one another, it's special. I've never felt like this in my life. And it's so much fun!"

"Are you saying you're infatuated with Juni and me?" I ask with raised eyebrows.

Asher looks serious and answers, "Not really. I think it's more than that. I know this is crazy talk because I've only been around you both for a short time, but I feel this strong draw to both of you. Like this is something profoundly different, and I need to explore it with you."

"That's incredibly sweet, don't you think, Jack?" When I look at Juni—probably with a crazed expression—she adds, "I feel the same way Asher does. This is great. When can we see each other again?" She looks closely at me and continues,

"Jack, are you okay about it? You seem a little dazed." She gently takes my hand, and Asher lays his enormous paw on my thigh. It feels possessive rather than comforting, but I like it tremendously.

I open my mouth to speak, but for a moment nothing comes out. Juni is beginning to look disappointed, so I blurt out, "I'm always the one who falls too quickly, but I'm so crazy about the two of you, I can hardly believe it. I've been trying to tell myself to be cool, but you're both so different from the people I've been dating. I hope I'm not deluded, but I feel like I can trust you not to break my heart. Can I? Please tell me honestly. My tender heart can only take so much after what happened a while back when a girlfriend I was serious about ghosted me. Since then, I haven't been able to trust myself."

"Sorry about your bad experience, but I'm not going to be the one to break this up, I promise," Asher says, completely flooring me with his conviction. "I've been wishing for years I could find this type of connection with someone, and here I feel it with two people. It's like… perfection."

"That's amazing, Asher," Juni says, and I swear I see stars in her eyes. "I hope this is as real as it feels right now. I'm blown away by you guys." She asks again, "When can I see you both? I hope it's soon."

"Tomorrow would be good for me if you would like to come out to the campground. I have my own cabin there, and the new group isn't arriving until Monday morning around ten, so we'll basically have the place to ourselves. I could even provide horses if you want to go on a trail ride in the woods. Do you ride? The horses are gentle, and we trust them with newbies all the time."

I laugh and tell him, "Where I grew up, serious riding lessons were expected. I know my way around a horse. I need to get some work done in the morning for an upcoming show, but I can take off tomorrow afternoon. My assistant can manage the gallery for an afternoon. We're closed on Mondays."

"Juni?" he asks.

"I haven't ridden for years, but I know the basics. I probably won't disgrace myself. It sounds like fun, Asher. Thanks! Sundays and Mondays are my days off, so this will work."

"Great. Come out to the camp around two. I'll show you around and then we can saddle up the horses. You can ride Western or English, though we have more Western tack for the campers. Do either of you have a preference?"

"Western for me," Juni answers. "Those English saddles look too skimpy." Asher and I get a chuckle out of that observation.

"I've ridden a lot more hunt seat, but I'm fine with anything," I tell them.

Asher smiles and continues, "Okay, you can pick out what you want when you get there. Most of the horses are versatile, and a couple of them are decent jumpers if you want to try that. I'll have the cook pull together a picnic for us, and we can ride out to a picturesque spot I know and have our supper there. We can even cool off in the pond if you're up for it. It's completely secluded."

"That sounds like fun," Juni says. "Where is the camp?"

"If you head out of town past the hat factory, keep going for about half a mile, and you'll see Beehive Drive on your right. Take that and it'll lead you right to the camp. Park in the lot and text me if I'm not already outside waiting. I'll come get you."

They check that they have each other's number from the group text I sent. It's so businesslike to me all of a sudden, and my insecurities mount until they both wrap their arms around me simultaneously. Juni buries her face in my chest while Asher tells me, "Thanks for having us over tonight, Jack. I think you've started something really important for us." He kisses me, then kisses Juni, who in turn kisses me too, and my worries evaporate—for now anyway.

I try to believe my inner monsters won't rise up to annoy me a few times before I see them again, but it's not working as well as I'd like. I wish I could be as confident as Asher.

"Has anyone ever broken your heart?" I ask him suddenly.

Asher's face clouds and his blissed-out expression disappears. "Yes," he says in a flat tone. "Not in the way you probably imagine. It's not something I normally talk about, so let's not ruin our perfect evening with that story, alright?"

"Sure. Sorry. It's just that you're so sure of yourself, and I'd love to feel that confident."

"You will, Jack. Just trust us. Juni and I will guard your heart."

"Aww," Juni says and kisses him. "You're about the sweetest man I've ever met, Asher." She kisses him again and looks thoughtful. "Have you guys ever taken the hat factory tour? I hear it's fascinating, and tourists routinely make it part of their trip when they come here. Do you know why?"

I know this town's history, so I pipe up. "I've taken the tour. It was an abandoned factory, and Governor Lassiter's younger sister Madison refurbished it to make hats. She's done such an incredible job with the business, and she's expanded the factory to about three times its original size. Her flagship boutique is over in Louisville, but they now have a boutique in the factory as well, and she wholesales hats all over the world to fancy shops. She and her brother are Honeybee Hollow success stories. Madison's husband Halden Dahl is a famous glass artist, and he's built an incredible stained-glass window in the boutique depicting the history of hats. It's amazing and just another reason Honeybee Hollow is so sought after for a vacation destination. Halden is going to do a blown glass exhibit in my gallery in a few months, and I couldn't be happier about it."

"Well, I'm sure glad we all ended up moving here," Juni says.

"Me too," Asher agrees.

Asher stifles a yawn, and we all smile. It's been a long, enjoyable evening, but it's time to say good night.

I can't wait for tomorrow, but I wonder if Dr. Alister—I mean Weston—would mind it if I called him. Not tonight, of course.

♡♡♡

In the morning, I rush downstairs and get my work done in a quarter of the time I usually take, then I send him a text so I'm hopefully not bothering him.

> Jack Hartz: Wow, last night was better than I could have ever imagined. Thank you for boosting my confidence.

> Weston Alister: Hang on. Calling in a minute.

I can't suppress the smile in my voice when I answer the phone, "Hi Doc."

"Jack! I'm so glad to hear you're doing well. Tell me about them."

"They are both absolutely wonderful, and we really might have something special going on. We're trying to take things slowly, but I'm seeing them again today. I don't know what's going to happen, but we have an outdoorsy day and evening planned. After that… I'm not sure."

"That sounds terrific. I mean it though, if you run into any problems or need to clear your head, give me a call. And another thing… I… ah… hope you don't mind. I mentioned to my partners that one of my clients was considering a ménage, and they both recommended we send you a list of a few books you might want to read. They're romances, not how-to books, so the sex scenes are a bit idealized, but you might get some ideas and pointers from them. And they're fun reading. You can even share them with your partners if you like. Load up your Kindle and have a ball."

"Wow, thanks, Doc…"

"Weston."

"Right. Thanks, Weston. This means a lot. You're the best."

In a couple of minutes, a list arrives via text, and I do my Amazon shopping. I can't wait to jump in and read one by Dolly Gunn that sounds especially good. It's called *Two Plus Me.* This results in me forgetting to eat lunch because I'm so engrossed. This is hot stuff! By the time I'm ready to set the book aside, it's almost one, and I'm not at all ready to go. So I dash around for a while pulling myself together. I wolf down a peanut butter sandwich, pull on my breeches and boots— happy to go riding again—and briefly consider taking a bathing suit to swim in. Asher said the pond was secluded, though, so I think he meant swimming attire was optional. I go a little wild here and leave the swimsuit. Maybe I'll set a trend.

Heading out to the campground, I wonder about the kinds of people who show up there for corporate bonding experiences and retreats. I can't imagine what it must be like to work at a huge company. I love my gallery and being able to make my own decisions.

As I drive past the hat factory, I smile at how the Lassiters put this sleepy little burg nestled in the Appalachian Mountains on the map. I never would have heard of it and brought my girlfriend here if it hadn't been for their amazing successes.

I banish the memory of being ghosted by her for the thousandth time. There's nothing to be done for it, and it only serves to make me feel awful. It's time to have fun with Asher and Juni.

Eight

OUR DAY AT HONEYCOMB CAMP IS EVERYTHING WE COULD have hoped for. The grounds are beautiful, and we take off on three sweet horses who clearly know where to go without much coaxing from us. Asher leads us along a shady trail until he's sure Juni is comfortable and then speeds up wherever the terrain is safe enough. He shows us a place where I can take a jump over a downed log, but Juni can take a detour around it. I don't mind showing off a little.

When the terrain turns rougher, he tells us we'll have to slow down and walk a while and let the horses relax. The whole time, Asher keeps up a soliloquy about native plants and trees we pass with fascinating anecdotes about the medicinal properties—both real and assumed—of many of them. I bet he'd have made a great professor if he could have taught his classes outdoors. I guess there aren't too many places where you can do that year-round, however.

Finally, we reach our destination where a serene pond spreads out reflecting the mountains in its still water. The only noises besides our horses' hoofbeats are buzzing insects and bird calls.

"This looks like paradise," I exclaim to my friends, and Asher chuckles.

"You're not the first to make that observation—it's actually called Paradise Pond."

Juni laughs too and says, "I figured with being located in Honeybee Hollow, it would be called something like The Land of Milk and Honey."

We dismount and lead the horses over to the water's edge to take a long drink, and then we take off their saddles and tie them up to a hitching rail someone—no doubt Asher—thoughtfully installed nearby in the shade. It's still bright because it's only early evening, and the temperature is pretty warm and humid. Asher shows us the ice chest he stowed near the horses.

"I drove out here earlier and stashed all of our food and drinks. There's a road through there," he tells us indicating a grove of trees. "It's a much more direct route by truck, but not as scenic, so I thought you'd like the ride."

"It was great, Asher," Juni says.

"It was," I tell him. "It feels so good to ride again. It's been too long."

"Just let me know whenever you'd like to take a horse out for a spin," he says with a smile. "They always need exercise because not all of the camp experiences include them." He looks at us. "Anyone up for a cooling-off swim?" As he says this, Asher begins to remove his clothes. He is the most incredible specimen of masculine perfection ever. "I also brought towels and a blanket to sit on for when we're done swimming." By now he's completely in the buff and takes off for the water without a backward glance. His all-over tan tells me he does this often.

Juni and I both admire Asher's retreating form and then look at each other. She smiles and shrugs, and we both begin to strip. Apparently, I was right to leave the swimsuit. We grab each other's hands and head to the water's edge where Asher took off. He's already swimming around in deeper water.

"Hurry up you two!" he calls with a laugh. "We'll need to eat soon so we can leave before the mosquitos get bad and it's too dark to see the trail."

"Ah, good thinking," I answer. We don't exactly have headlights on the horses, and the trail isn't lit.

"Wow!" Juni says with a laugh as we step into the water. "This feels warmer than I expected, but it's still brisk."

I take a minute to enjoy watching her pick her way into the water, avoiding the large rocks in her way. She looks like she belongs in this idyllic setting as much as Asher does. How did

I get to be so lucky? Finally, I join them in the middle of the pond. It's not deep. I find I can stand up and keep my head out of the water. No doubt that's one of the reasons it's so warmed by the sun. I was relieved it didn't feel like ice water.

"How often do you swim here, Asher?" I ask.

"As often as possible. It's one of my favorite places to just come and chill out at the end of a long day. I've never brought anyone else here, though."

"Not even the campers?"

"Hah, no. Especially not them. I'd be afraid they'd want to come back all the time and spoil it. It's like my own private oasis. The camp has lots of other places we can take people to on horseback where they can have a cookout or whatever."

"I feel special," Juni says softly.

"You are," he responds. "Both of you."

My heart suddenly has that full feeling I experienced last night, so I sidle closer and put my arms around them. "Thank you for such a beautiful day, Asher." We all squeeze together, and the sensation of refreshing water and warm, naked flesh surrounding me is almost too good. "This is definitely paradise," I whisper.

We all kiss for a while and rub our bodies together in a most tantalizing way until Asher regretfully pulls back and says, "Let's keep the good stuff for later when we're back in the cabin. I wasn't joking about the mosquitos. If we want to have more au naturel fun in the future, we'll have to get an earlier start." Then he gives us both affectionate pats on the butt and wades to the shore. "Watch your step climbing out." He reaches a hand toward Juni as she navigates around some rocks again. Once more the sight of the two of them takes my breath away. They're just that perfect.

"Come on, Jack," he calls. "Quit horndogging at Juni's cute butt." He grabs a handful of said butt as she chuckles.

Still naked as a jaybird, Asher grabs his stash of towels and a big blanket that he spreads out on the grass. He then opens the cooler and produces beer and scrumptious-looking sandwiches. My stomach growls in appreciation. As Juni and I dry off, Asher settles down on the blanket and pulls more goodies out for us. He has chips, fruit, and brownies. I briefly consider putting some clothes back on, but shrug at Juni as we make the silent agreement to "when in Rome" go to dinner in the buff with our hedonistic host.

"I feel so decadent," I tell them as I admire the water droplets drizzling down Asher's chest from his wet hair. He didn't feel the need to dry off. It's a strange sensation to lie in the presence of two naked bodies and sport a semi-hard-on while eating a tasty meal. Apparently, Juni and I have the same effect on Asher. Surely, we can deflate these stiffies before we get back on our horses. What an uncomfortable thought.

We're all unable to stop touching one another. Silky caresses, feeding each other tasty bits of food, leaning into each other, hands touching hands—over and over we make what looks like incidental contact, but each time we do it, it feels like a promise.

"I'm just going to say, you guys," Juni tells us, "I think we're making something magical here together. How can this feel *so* right… and *so quickly*?"

Asher is swift to answer, "When something is really right, you just know. And we just know."

"My therapist is pretty jazzed for us," I tell them. "He even recommended some interesting reading for us to enjoy. I started reading one of the books earlier today and got so wrapped up in it, I was almost late getting here. Apparently, there is a whole genre in romance books that talk about the kind of relationship we're building. They call it MMF. It makes for steamy reading, that's for sure." I clear my throat and look at them. "Are we ready yet for some more serious stuff when we get back to the cabin?"

"I am," Juni answers with conviction.

"That's what I like to hear," Asher says. "The real thing."

"So you're both ready for some fucking?"

They look at each other and grin. "Yes," they answer simultaneously.

Juni shivers a little and laughs softly. "I'm so turned on right now, you two. You have no idea. I bet I'd shock the pants off most of my women friends if I told anyone about this."

Okay, that doesn't sound right to me. "Does this embarrass you, Juni? Are you ashamed of having two lovers at once?"

"Oh, heavens no. I'm sorry if I sounded like that. I just

mean we're pretty unusual, and I'm going to have to figure out how to deal with it around other people. Frankly, I think my parents would be completely cool with it because I suspect they've dabbled in polyamory. It's my girlfriends who aren't always as open-minded and might feel funny about it—the ones who aren't green with jealousy. But ultimately this is my decision, and I choose you two over anyone who has a problem with us."

That sounds better.

"Ready to head back?" Asher asks with a broad grin.

"You bet," I answer.

"Absolutely," Juni agrees. "Oh, and I did a little reading myself," she adds with a wink. "I have plans for you two."

Sadly, we all get back into our clothes. I miss the sight of all that beautiful flesh on display. Then we clean up the remains of our picnic and saddle the horses, who seem to have had a nice nap.

I hope we can do this often; what a treat. I don't remember the last time I felt so relaxed and happy. But now a current of excitement and anticipation is beginning to zing through me.

Nine

ASHER

My two partners are so beautiful and amazing, and I can't wait to get these horses to the paddock and get Juni and Jack out of their clothes again. Too bad it would have been a poor idea to reenact Lady Godiva's famous ride on our way back to camp. I'd have loved to see Juni's tits bouncing and her bare ass jiggling on the back of her horse. But I'm a gentleman, so I didn't suggest anything untoward. Besides, we certainly don't need saddle sores in all the wrong places. And… I'm feeling horribly possessive about these two right now and wouldn't want any of the employees to catch sight of them.

When we hit camp, we take care of the horses, and I make

sure they're fed and have fresh water. Then we head up to my cabin, making a detour for Juni and Jack to pick up their overnight bags from their cars. My cabin is rustic from the outside, but the inside never fails to surprise visitors. It's modern and incredibly nice inside with excellent heat and air conditioning so I can live here year-round in complete comfort. I have a small kitchen for when I don't want to eat in the dining hall, and the rest of the layout is open in design. The most important thing is that I have a delightfully huge bed under a skylight. I love seeing the stars at night, and I wake up with the sun on most days. Right now, the skylight is glowing pinkish orange as the sun is going down.

Next to the bed is a large box of condoms and a bottle of lube. I'm such a boy scout. Always prepared.

"Anyone feel like a quick shower?" I know they will, so without waiting for an answer, I lead them to the bathroom and wait for the inevitable gasps. There is a closeted room for the toilet, but the shower that takes up most of the room is next to a walled garden visible through an enormous window. It's completely private but makes you feel as if you're showering outside.

"Wow," Jack says in the awed voice I expected.

Juni gasps too and asks, "Did you design this? It's breathtaking."

I can't hide my pride. "I designed it and built it. Tore open the house, installed the sliding glass door, built the garden wall with a securely locking gate, and landscaped all of the plantings. Every plant is native to Kentucky, and all are either edible or have medicinal properties. I may have switched jobs, but I'm still a botanist." I'm tempted to point out my favorites, but then decide it's not time for a lecture. Instead, I turn on the ceiling-mounted rainfall showerhead and adjust the water. Right on cue, my eager guests start to shuck their clothes.

"This is like being back at the pond," Jack comments as he steps into the shower with me. "You're so at one with nature, Asher. And it makes me even more in awe of you knowing that you designed this."

"It's no more impressive than your gallery or Juni's coffee house. We all have our special talents. And tonight we can all explore our… other talents." I reach for Jack and pull him to me. Our naked bodies slam together, and I'm instantly hard. Jack is as well, as I kiss him deeply. Our cocks rub one another lusciously.

"Oh wow," Juni whispers. "You two are so hot together. I can't get enough of the sight. You're so beautiful and yet completely masculine at the same time."

I notice she begins to pluck her nipples and squeeze her legs together. I'm suddenly ravenous for both of them. I reach for her too and announce, "I want to fuck both of you so badly right now. I swear to God I wish I had two dicks."

Juni chuckles and I feel a shiver go through Jack. He looks deeply into my eyes and says, "I'm vers, but I really enjoy being a bottom. Well, except for with women. I *love* fucking women."

"Hot damn," I say. "That sounds just right. You fuck Juni, and I'll fuck you at the same time. It'll be like I'm fucking the two of you at once, and we all ought to be happy, right?"

"No complaints from me," Jack offers with another shiver, and Juni grins from ear to ear as she nods vigorously. I think I hear a little squeak come out of her, but I'm not sure.

"Well, let's get cleaned up so we can get dirty again." I grab some body wash that reminds me of pine trees and fresh snow and start to soap them up. We all lather each other in a big soapy, bubbly free-for-all. There's nothing like stroking your lovers over and over with their skin all slick and warm and punctuating each caress with a deep kiss. The contrast of kissing Juni and then switching immediately to Jack's face is amazing. She's all soft and smooth where Jack has a lovely scratchy scruff that rasps my face delightfully. I can't get enough of them.

Once we're refreshed and thoroughly rinsed, I grab some big towels for them, and we head to the bed. "Tonight is going to change things for us," I tell them as I kiss gently up and down Juni's long, graceful neck. "Last chance to bail."

She gives me a fake shocked look and exclaims, "Not on your life when my lifelong dream of being with two men is about to be fulfilled." Then she laughs. "Well, maybe not exactly *lifelong*, but certainly post-high-school." As she says this, Jack has pressed himself against her from behind and reaches around with both hands. One fondles a nipple and the other slides between her legs. She lets out another little squeak.

I'm beginning to love that noise.

We all pile onto the bed then, and we're a mass of stroking hands and busy lips. At one point, Jack and I alternate between kissing each other and licking Juni's sweet pussy. We probe her together with joined fingers as Jack sucks her clit into his mouth. With a cry, Juni's hips levitate off the bed, and she lands writhing with what appears to be a most satisfying orgasm. She squirms and moans until I can't stand it and have to also suck her sensitive clit into my mouth. I lash it back and forth with my tongue as Juni makes all sorts of appreciative noises and grasps my hair. That little squeak of hers has morphed into a drawn-out wail by the time we're done with her. Her chest heaves and she's glassy-eyed, but she begs anyway, "Jack, please, I need you to fuck me now and fuck me hard!" She reaches out as if to grab him by his dick, but he has momentarily stepped away toward the bedside table.

"Yes, ma'am!" he says with a laugh and grabs a condom. Within seconds he's suited up and climbing over Juni. He plunges deep within her as he begins—ramming over and over, to the hilt. He's rougher than I expected, and it makes me groan.

Juni has a strong grip on his hips, encouraging him to go faster. "Yes, like that!"

Putting a gentle hand on his shoulder, I caution, "Slow

down, buddy. You don't want to come so fast you miss the rest of the action here."

Jack glances back over his shoulder and blushes. "She just feels *so* perfect, Asher. It's like heaven inside of her. Just you wait." But he relaxes and slows down his thrusts so I can get him ready for me. I kiss his muscular ass and stroke his seam. All lubed up, I begin to probe him gently with my finger. Jack tenses for a second until I breach his entrance, and he sighs, "Ahh, yes! More of that please, Asher."

Within a minute, I'm up to prodding him with three well-lubed fingers, and his muscles contract and relax around me so hard, I know he's going to feel like he's swallowing me up. I can't wait a second longer. I roll on a condom and position myself behind Jack. Then I ease my dick into him. This is so close to total perfection, I'm speechless. The only thing that would make it better would be if we ditched the condoms.

When I'm all the way into Jack's hot body, he throws back his head and shouts, "Yes, Asher! I love it! Fuck me! Ohmygod, I'm fucking you both at once." His chest is heaving, and he's breaking into a sweat.

Juni's eyes are glued to Jack's face, and they're sparkling with happiness. Then she shifts her gaze briefly to mine and whispers, "Thank you."

I have no idea why I deserve thanks. This is hands-down the hottest thing I've ever done. It makes my previous threesome mediocre fumbling in comparison. But now I am fully invested in the happiness of these new partners, and their arousal makes me hotter than a burnt marshmallow over a campfire. I plow into Jack, who in turn rams into Juni, whose eyes roll back as she makes an indecipherable noise.

Jack lets out a series of satisfied growls as I grind against his prostate while gripping his hips like a vise. I can't keep myself from kissing and then nipping his neck. Something profound comes over me suddenly and I blurt out, "I'm falling in love with you two!" Where did *that* come from? I've never said that to a soul in my life. But it's *true*.

Juni's eyes fly open, and the most beautiful smile greets me.

Jack turns his face to the side so I can crane around and kiss his lips. When I'm done, he whispers, "Yeah, me too."

Well, I certainly didn't expect that, and I'm tremendously relieved neither of them laugh at me.

I redouble my efforts and fuck Jack like my life depends on it. An impending orgasm is creeping up on me, but I try to keep it at bay. "Is anyone else close?" I ask in a strangled voice.

Juni shudders and blinks as she groans, "I'm coming again now."

Jack nods, "Almost there, Asher. Just… right there… oh yesss," and he moans out the sexiest sound I've ever heard from a man.

This makes me feel free, so I let it happen and jerk as I empty what feels like my life savings into the condom. Over and over, I let it all go.

It's bliss—a white-hot, nearly religious experience.

I collapse onto Jack, who collapses onto Juni, who sighs, "Never have I ever… Oh, so good." Then she adds, "Yeah, I'm feeling it too, you guys. It's profound."

The only reason Jack or I need or want to get up is to get rid of the condoms, but we make it right back to the bed as quickly as possible and snuggle into a satisfied heap, pulling the blanket over us. Looking up through the skylight, I point out, "We have a full moon tonight."

"Perfect," Juni purrs in a sleepy voice.

It's not hard to sleep with them, I find. Sure, we have arms and legs everywhere because we're not small people, but touching them is a comfort. Jack starts out in the middle, but we shift around a few times as we wake and begin to stroke and kiss one another. At one point I end up fucking Juni while Jack alternately licks her clit or my dick.

He was right about her pussy feeling like heaven. She has muscles that… whew. Clever Jack lubes up his fingers and plays with both of our assholes at the same time as I fuck her, and I have to say, it's an amazing experience. Like I said—he can multitask really well, so we reward him by giving him a dual blowjob. I have a whole new appreciation for threesomes now that I'm conscious of wanting to please both of them and feel their affection for me expressed in each stroke, kiss, or thrust. My God, this is fun. But there's also something completely profound about it. I'm so relieved they weren't freaked out by my admission earlier. And I'm feeling it even more strongly now.

Finally, after I've come—I don't know how many times—we collapse into deep sleep and don't wake until the sunlight shines bright on us through the skylight. I scrub my eyes and sit up to check the clock, groaning when I realize I have new campers coming in about an hour. I need to feed Juni and Jack, then get a move on. Nudging them, I say softly, "We need to get up. The new group is about to arrive."

We all head back into the shower and wash up a lot faster than last night. Looking at one another, we all notice a bit of beard burn, faint bite marks, and a couple of scratches here and there. All in all, the marks of some serious fun.

Ultimately Juni and Jack let me get ready for the new arrivals without getting in my way, even though I tried to reassure them everything would be alright. I watch their cars pull out of the campground with a surprising amount of sadness.

But then the chartered bus shows up early, and it's showtime—no matter what. I scoot into the dining hall and grab a coffee and breakfast sandwich from the cook, thanking her profusely.

I have to force some smiles today, not only because I miss my lovers. I didn't even give them a proper kiss goodbye.

Ten

"How about breakfast at Hot Stuff?" I ask Jack as we head to our cars. "It's closed for business, and we'll have the place to ourselves. Anything you want is on the house."

"Sounds perfect," Jack tells me. "I'm starving."

We head to town, and I let Jack in through the back door. I brew us some coffee and then we proceed to make our way through an enormous breakfast.

"That was pretty amazing last night, Jack. But do you think Asher is serious about his feelings? It's pretty soon to be declaring himself. I hope he wasn't just trying to make us feel good."

"I understand your concern, but I also have a strong

feeling that he was being sincere. I know how hard it is to open up to someone."

"Have you ever been in love, Jack?"

He looks down at his coffee for a moment and clears his throat. "I have, actually," he says softly, and I have an immediate need to reach out and hold his hand. His beautiful face is suddenly the picture of sadness. "After that ended—rather horribly—I started… pushing myself to love. I fooled myself over and over, convincing myself that I had strong feelings for all the wrong people. It was like I *had* to be in love to be happy, but I had no ability anymore to evaluate people. That's why I started consulting with my therapist. He's been helping me make better decisions. But strangely, when I called to talk to him about you and Asher, he could tell this was different, and he told me to go for it." The sadness clears from his eyes, and he looks at me so sweetly.

I smile back. "Who were you in love with, if you don't mind me asking?"

"I had a girlfriend named Blakelee when I lived in Lexington. We drove over here to Honeybee Hollow for a weekend getaway, and I decided right then and there I wanted to sell my place and move here to open a gallery. She seemed at the time to be one hundred percent on the same page and was looking forward to working with me in the gallery. She was also supposedly an art lover. So, I bought the building on Third Street and made all sorts of plans for it. She was quite helpful and seemed to be as excited as I was, although in retrospect, I wonder if I missed some signs that she wasn't. I really don't know." He takes a deep breath. "Anyway, I packed up my belongings when it was time to make the move. We planned that she would bring her stuff in her own car in the next week or so, depending on how quickly she could pack. I had to meet with contractors, or I'd have stayed longer to help. We spoke a couple of times after that, but then she stopped answering my calls." Jack frowns into the distance, clearly remembering. I slide my hand across to take his. "She never showed up. I was scared to death that something had happened to her. I called and called, and then one day, the phone didn't even do so much as ring. She blocked me!"

"What a chicken shit way to act," I can't help saying to him. Who could be so mean to Jack? He's such a sweetheart.

"Yeah, it was, but I finally got through to her best friend. I was so panicked that something had happened, and I talked myself into thinking her phone had been damaged in an accident rather than she'd blocked me. Her friend coldly told me to leave her out of it and catch a clue that Blakelee didn't want to see me anymore. I don't know what happened, but my imagination has come up with lots of crazy ideas. Once I knew she was okay, I stopped calling, of course. But I just couldn't understand what changed."

"I can imagine. I'm so sorry, Jack. That must have hurt."

"It hurt like hell for a long time, but you and Asher are so special to me, I don't ache inside anymore. I really am falling for both of you, and I trust you both with my heart."

I can't help it. Since we didn't get much sleep last night, I let out a colossal yawn and give him a sheepish smile. "Jack, you are the sweetest, dearest man, and I feel the same way about you. And Asher. Would you like to come upstairs and take a nap with me? I don't think he would mind, do you?"

"I wouldn't mind if you took one with him, and I hope jealousy won't be an issue, but we could always let him know."

"Excellent idea." So I fire off a text to Asher and immediately get the answer that he's not at all jealous of us being together and hopes we can manage to still have fun without him. He also says he'll be done by eight p.m., and he'd love to see us tonight. After showing the text to Jack, we make plans to meet one another after dinner above Imagine Gallery because Jack has a bigger bed. Mine is too small for three, but Jack and I have a lovely nap with just the two of us.

AND THIS IS HOW WE LEAD OUR LIVES FOR THE NEXT FEW months. We learn everything we can about one another. Jack told Asher the same story about his past, but we also found out he comes from a wealthy family with parents who spend a lot of time traveling. That wasn't too hard to guess. I do wonder sometimes whether Jack's strong need to be loved comes from feeling abandoned by his parents who have always been on the move without him.

My story is the least interesting. Hippie parents who've dabbled in everything and found their true calling with their restaurant. I got out from under their influence when I could because I wanted something of my own, even though I love them dearly.

Interestingly, none of us has any siblings.

But Asher is the one with the craziest background. He told us his story one night after a particularly passionate session of lovemaking, and we were all feeling emotional.

"I was raised in an obscure religious cult in Indiana. My parents, who met when my father was a missionary to American Samoa, were strictly fundamental about their beliefs and told me many times I'd been born a sinner because I 'ruined' my mother's ability to have more children. I always felt awful about that as a kid and tried to do everything perfectly to atone for my evils. As I grew older and spent more time on my own in the library, I read enough to know what they said was a lot of manipulative garbage. I didn't like being controlled at all, so I began to act out. But my birth disaster was my first sin.

"My second major sin happened when I was around sixteen, I announced to them I was gay, although I knew I liked girls. I thought it would get a bigger rise out of them than admitting to bisexuality. They were completely appalled and sent me away to a camp for reprogramming, and although I hated everything about the camp's message, I adored the setting. It was in a beautiful forest, so I'd sneak off daily to go and observe the fascinating plants there. The administrators got so sick of searching for me all the time, they sent me home, but my interest in nature and plants solidified in my head. My parents were furious with me and livid with the camp for not 'fixing' me.

"My third horrible sin and the one that severed our relationship irreparably was that instead of working to become a preacher in their strange cult—as they'd planned for me since birth—I managed to get a scholarship to Purdue to study science. *That* was blasphemy. I packed my bag, hitched a ride to campus, and my parents never spoke to me again. They have shunned me. So, even though they literally named me 'gift from God,' I no longer exist to them."

This story hurts. How can parents turn their back on such a perfect human being as Asher? He's talented and caring, generous, and adores everything about the world except for bigotry. He would love his parents back if they could try to at least acknowledge his existence. Jack and I shower him with even more love after this conversation. No wonder he said his heart had been broken in an unusual way.

We all have busy schedules, but we make each other a priority without worry that anyone is being left out. Sometimes one of us ends up alone for a night for one reason or another, and we just move along. It's fine.

Until it's not.

Eleven

IT'S A COLD, RAINY SUNDAY AFTERNOON, AND WE'RE relaxing at my place with a cozy fire going in my antique wood-burning stove. Juni and I have both added extra help to our businesses, so we all have more time to spend with each other now. This is also the slow season for Asher because people only come down to the camp for limited stays in the middle of winter.

The coffee table has bowls of chips and pretzels to munch on, and we're drinking delicious craft beer. Every so often we pay attention to the football game on TV. It's more fun to snuggle, but the game is supposed to be a great match-up, according to Asher. The winner will go to the Super Bowl, so we cheer and drink beer when either team scores or makes a good play. I can't even keep the teams straight, frankly. One name has something to do with horses and the other with birds, but that's all I remember. The Studs and the Buzzards? I dunno… something like that… maybe. At least they're playing someplace warm. Or maybe it's indoors. Heck if I know.

It's the third quarter, and the score is tied twenty-one to twenty-one. The horse team has the ball and looks like they have a good chance of making a touchdown when there is a knock on my door. We must have been making too much noise to hear someone coming up the steps, but the horsey guys had made an excellent long pass and great reception, and we had to do some cheering and drinking about it.

I look at Juni and Asher. "Did either of you order pizza or something?"

"Nope."

"Not me." Juni asks, "Are you going to answer that?"

Shrugging, I sigh, "I guess."

I make my way to the door, hoping there isn't a problem in the gallery, and open it to a shocking blast of cold air. A woman is standing there clothed in a hooded raincoat and dragging a sopping suitcase with one hand and a huge purse with the other. I can barely see her under her hood because she's looking down. She's shivering, and I can hardly blame her. It's miserable out there in this torrential storm, and the rain has turned to sleet.

Just as I say, "Can I help you?" she raises her face up to me and either she's spent a lot of time out in the rain, or she's been crying. Her face is streaming with water.

My mouth falls open. "Blakelee? What are you doing here?"

"C-can I p-please come in?"

My inborn manners kick in and I step back, completely nonplussed. "Yes, of course, let's get you inside where it's warm." I'm shocked I could get the words out because my mouth is suddenly as dry as a saltine cracker. *What the hell is she doing here?*

She steps inside with water and ice crystals cascading all around her onto my floor. Her boots are splattered with mud, and she looks bedraggled. I'm not at all happy to have her inside my home. Given our history, I'd very much love to tell her to turn around and take a long drive back to anywhere but here, but she's obviously soaked through and freezing. I was not raised to be that callous.

"Do you mind leaving the boots here by the door? I'll go hang your coat in the shower to dry."

She nods and peels off her things. She isn't dressed for this kind of weather at all. The coat and boots were crucial to her well-being because underneath she's wearing her favorite dress—one she knew I used to like on her. It made her tits look like a million bucks. It's quite short and definitely more of a summer sundress than an outfit for a winter storm. Why would she show up in such a dumb getup in this weather?

As I rush by Asher and Juni with the dripping coat, they stare at me, questioning. I try to convey as much as possible in my wide-eyed look, flattened mouth, and double-shoulder shrug. I have no idea what to say to anyone right now. I dump the coat in the shower and go back into my room to look for a hanger, and I overhear Juni growl loudly, "So… *you're* Blakelee. We know all about you and how you've treated Jack. I hope you're not here to try something. He's taken."

Wow. So much for subtlety. My heart swells at her pronouncement.

Then I hear Asher's voice soothing Juni's ruffled feathers, though I can't hear the words. Blakelee hasn't said a thing.

I quickly hang up the coat and head back into the living room. Blakelee hasn't moved away from the door, where she's still shaking. "Care to have a seat?" I ask. "Or would you prefer to put on some real clothes?" I glance at her dripping suitcase and hope it's not ruining my hardwood floor.

Heading for the kitchen, I grab a towel that I hand her. She starts to wipe her face with it when I say, "It's for that soaking, filthy luggage you brought in. Please don't make a mess of my house."

I suppose I should offer her a hot drink, but somehow, I can't seem to muster up much in the way of caring about her right now. I stare at her a moment and then say, "You're probably waiting for me to ask you what you're doing here, but honestly, I don't care. And if you're expecting to stay, you're not welcome, and there's no room."

Blakelee inhales sharply and asks, "May I use your bathroom to put on some warmer clothes?"

"That makes a lot more sense than showing up like this," I say, indicating her stupid dress. I glance outside at my thermometer and say, "It's thirty degrees right now. What were you thinking?" Then I give her a stern look and tell her, "Once you're more properly dressed, there is an inn up the street you should check into if you're planning on taking in the sights of the town. It's a lovely place to *visit*."

"I hoped maybe we could…uh… talk a little after I change."

"I'm busy."

"You're just watching football," she splutters. "You don't even like football."

"I like it just fine. Lots of things are different now, but maybe you didn't notice that I'm not alone, and I'd like to get back to my friends."

From the couch, Juni lets out a snort and asks, "Friends, huh?" She doesn't sound too happy with that description of our relationship. I'm messing up rather badly.

Asher strokes her head and gives her a little kiss, whispering something that makes her smile. He stands and extends his hand to Blakelee, saying, "Asher Bellamy, Jack's boyfriend, and this is Juniper Barry, *our* girlfriend." He clasps her limp hand and continues, "I guess you're Blakelee, the vicious ex who ghosted our man. Thanks for that, by the way, the three of us have never been happier." Blakelee snatches her hand out of his massive grip. This is not going well, but I really don't care.

Blakelee stalks off to the bathroom, dragging her nasty suitcase behind her. I grab a mop from the utility closet and clean up the trail of water and mud she leaves behind. Apparently, she parked her car in the unpaved lot up the street instead of parking in front of the gallery, and I wonder why. I take a peek out the front window, however, and see that all the spaces are full. Oops. Well, too bad for her. Good for business though. The Halden Dahl glass exhibit we have in the gallery is bringing in people in droves, and I've been terribly busy with it. It was nice to take today off and relax finally. After the article published in a statewide magazine about my gallery being one of the three hottest and trendiest in Kentucky, I've been doing amazingly well.

As soon as Blakelee is out of earshot, Juni says, "I assume you'd like some privacy to talk to her. Should Asher and I go over to my place and let you be?"

"I don't like the idea of you two walking over there, even if it's just a block away. It's awful outside, and I have a nice dinner planned for us. Well, nothing fancy, but I made spaghetti sauce. If Blakelee is so gung-ho about talking, and she has to have privacy—which I don't care about—maybe she and I could talk in the bedroom, and you can finish watching the game."

Asher grins and says, "Or better yet, Juni and I could take the bedroom and you two could stay out here and argue until you're sick of it, and then we'll come out and have dinner. I don't want to drag Juni out in this weather either." He chuckles and adds, "Don't worry, we could find something to do in there, and we'd even try to be quiet." He winks at me. "Or not."

"Honestly, I'd prefer if you both stayed in here. I don't particularly want to be alone with her, and I don't give a rat's ass about what she has to say. That ship sailed a long time ago."

Blakelee reappears in a low-cut pink sweater and gray slacks, both of which hug her curves like paint. She really is trying to get some point across with the clothes, but her attire is doing nothing for me. Frankly, neither is her body. Objectively, I know she's pretty, but I can't get past my anger and hurt.

She pauses and strikes a pose, as if to let everyone appreciate her beauty, but we all ignore her and stare at the football game like it's fascinating. I doubt one of us could say what the score is or who's ahead right now.

She approaches and looks around for where to sit. Juni, Asher, and I are taking up the couch, so she flops into a side chair that she turns to face us instead of the TV.

"Jack, can we talk—privately?"

"Talk away. I have nothing to say to you. I don't even know what you're doing here. I tried to talk to you a year ago, and you wouldn't, so either say your piece or get out of here."

A tear rolls down her face that I catch in my peripheral

vision. Maybe I'm being too harsh. "There's beer in the fridge if you're thirsty." See? I can be polite.

"You know I don't drink that stuff. It's going to give you a fat belly of you keep it up."

Juni pipes up, "Not with the kind of exercise he gets." She snorts softly and adds in a stage whisper, "every night."

Asher gives her a fake chastising look and asks me again, "Want us to leave you two alone?"

"Yes—" Blakelee answers.

Just at the same time as I say, "Nope. Like I said, it's not necessary."

"Well, you're going to want to hear me out at some point, and it might as well be now. I drove over four hours to get here from Lexington, you know."

"Well, that's clearly an exaggeration; it's not that far away. So talk," I say with a shrug. I wish she'd get it over with or leave. There isn't much she can say.

Asher and Juni pretend to be watching the game, so Blakelee takes a deep breath and starts talking.

"First of all, I'm really, really sorry, Jack. I know that ignoring your calls and not showing up like we'd planned was a bad move."

"Ya think?" Oops. I need to reel that in. It sounds as if I care.

"Yes. I couldn't feel worse about my actions. It was a childish move." She wrings her hands and continues. "After you left, I continued to pack, but my mother showed up at my place and said she'd heard some disturbing news about you."

I finally tear my eyes off the game and realize she's blushing as she says this. I can't imagine what news would have turned "I love you and want to live with you" into "I never want to speak to you again" in such a short time.

"This is kind of awful to say, Jack, and I wish you'd let me say it in private but…"

"Anything you have to say to me is going to be repeated to Juni and Asher anyway, so you may as well get it over with and save me the breath."

She stares at me a moment as if weighing her options and then begins, "Okay. Well… my mother said she'd heard rumors that you were gay. Her friend had seen you kiss some guy in public. I questioned her more and apparently, it was before we met."

"So? I told you when I met you I'm bi. That shouldn't have been any shock."

"Bi, yes, but my mother was convinced and drummed it into my head that there is no such thing as bisexual, and you were just using me as a prop to look respectable."

My blood is boiling, and Asher is glaring daggers at her. "*Respectable*? And you believed that? What is wrong with being bi and being honest about it? It's how I was born—how God made me! I never cheated on you, and I had no intention of doing that either. Just because someone is bisexual doesn't mean they can't make their own mind up and commit to someone they love. And it sure as hell doesn't mean they're lying about their sexuality, no matter what uninformed people think. Your mom is way off base, Blakelee, and I'm offended. I can't believe you fell for her bullshit. I would *never* use someone to make myself look better to people around me. I'm fine the way I am, and I don't need your mother's version of respectable!"

Blakelee flinches and clasps her hands tightly as tears dribble down her face. With a wobbly chin, she tells me, "My mom can be so persuasive, and she wouldn't let up about it. I'm so sorry to admit I started to wonder if she was right. I think, however, my parents were still afraid I'd sneak off in the middle of the night to get to you, so they sent me to visit my mom's youngest cousin for a few months in Italy to help her with her new baby. I'd already quit my job, so I guess they thought I'd do better far away for a while. At least the trip was kinda fun. But I'm so sorry, Jack."

"That still doesn't explain why you packed a bag and drove all the way over here to tell me this crap."

"I drove here because I still love you!"

"Right," I snort. "You have a weird way of showing it. More than a year's worth of silence is supposed to convince me you love me? And if your mom was so against me, how is it she never said anything or acted unfriendly to me when I was around her for your family dinners and whatnot?"

"It was apparently new information that she had. I'd never mentioned to her that you'd told me you were bi." She sniffles loudly, so I go grab a box of tissues from the kitchen and hand it to her. "I was nervous about leaving Lexington because I like it there and like being near my friends and family. So when she started to drum this doubt about you into my head, I couldn't face talking to you. I did eventually unblock you, but I guess by then you'd given up calling me."

"Phones work two ways, you know," Juni interjects and then raises her hands in a backing-off gesture. "Sorry, I'll keep out of it. It's none of my business."

"It *is* your business, Juni," I say. "You're a big part of my life now, and I trust you and Asher to never pull this kind of nonsense on me. Besides, when *your* parents visited last month, they were happy for all of us."

"Happy" is putting it mildly. They thought it was the coolest thing ever and took full credit for raising an open-minded daughter. They're probably bragging about it to all of their restaurant patrons.

Blakelee flinches at this statement. After a protracted silence, she asks, "Are you really involved with two people at once, Jack?"

"I'm *in love* with two people, Blakelee. And extremely happy about it." I don't miss the satisfied smirks on Juni's and Asher's faces.

"Well then, what am *I* supposed to do? I'm still very much in love with you! I just took a long time assessing my life and doing some research on bisexuality and decided you were telling me the truth all along, and my mother was finally, for once in her life, wrong about something important. My mom is even more willing to accept you after she read that article about you in *Kentucky's Best*. She told me she may have misjudged you."

"I'm sorry, Blakelee. That news about your mother is disturbing and a little too conveniently timed." She sounds like a real opportunist if you ask me. The magazine reporter did more research into my background than I expected, and my family's fortune was discussed. Obviously, they didn't check with me about this before printing it. But I don't elaborate on that with Blakelee. I tell her instead, "I loved you to pieces… at one time. But what you did obliterated that feeling. Squashed it like a bug and crushed me in the process."

"Couldn't you try to get it back again?"

"Why?"

"Because I love you so much, and I *need* you."

She's full-on ugly crying now, and I can't help but hurt for her. My icy resolve crumbles because I know how awful a broken heart feels. Plus, she's taken a big risk opening herself up in front of Asher and Juni. That has to be mortifying. I finally cave in and say, "Let's go talk in the bedroom." I stand and lead her away by the hand from the noise of the TV and the prying eyes and ears of my current lovers.

Twelve

ASHER

"WOW. WHAT DO YOU THINK THEY'RE DOING IN THERE?" I ask Juni. Her face is red, and she looks angry.

"I don't know, but I don't like that they left us to go talk alone. You don't think he could be considering a reconciliation with her, do you? That idea makes me sick."

"I agree." I take a deep, fortifying breath. "We need to trust Jack, I suppose, and know that he wouldn't abandon us for her. She's horrible."

"That woman is an immature, pathetic mess if you ask me, and she has some nerve crying about how much she *needs* Jack. She doesn't give a damn about anyone but herself. I'd like to spank her perky little bottom for being such a big baby and see how she likes it."

"Ooh, kinky today, Juni? I didn't know you were into that kind of thing."

Juni squinches up her face at me and says, "Yuck. That's not what I meant. I just think Little Miss Lookit-Me needs to grow up. She's a crybaby. I mean, she's pretty and all, but… oh gross."

"So you won't be asking her to join our ménage?"

Juni gives me a flat look that suddenly morphs into a much more devilish one. "We could try," she says. "I'm willing to bet she'd run the opposite direction."

"And what if she doesn't? Would you be willing to try adding another woman to our relationship? Jack might be able to accept her if she's willing. He did say he was in pretty deep with her at one point, and you yourself pointed out that she had a great body. Aren't you a little attracted? I know you have that curious streak in you, or you'd never have played with your former roommate."

"Well… I could think about it, but your eagerness is worrying me, Asher. Are Jack and I not enough for you? I'm just thinking of posing it to her so she'll get spooked and leave town."

"Juni, I love you. And I love Jack. You know that. You are both it for me, but because I love Jack so much, I'm willing to consider a change if—and only if—that is what he wants. I'm afraid he might leave us for her. He was all tough on the outside with her, but you know as well as I do she was starting to get to him. He's a big softy with a huge heart, and he loves love. He might be in there reconciling with her and didn't want to do it in front of us."

"So what should we do?"

"Let's give them some time to finish their conversation and then surprise them."

"Oh, I like that idea. You have a wonderful mind, Asher Bellamy. I love it."

We drink some more beer and finish watching the game. The ending was just what the sports prognosticators expected, so that was kinda boring. I stand to clean up the bottles and leftover munchies, and Juni wanders over to the window.

"Wow, look at this, Asher. There are tiny icicles all over the place now. I bet the roads are a mess." I join her, and sure enough, it's treacherous outside. The street is empty of both cars and people, so I'm glad to see folks paid attention and went home before it got this bad out there. This isn't our typical weather. "I'm not even sure," Juni says, "that any of us could get down Jack's steps this evening."

"Oh great. That means we could be stuck with Blakelee until the spring thaw."

"At least Jack made spaghetti and we won't go hungry. Maybe I'll go warm up the sauce on the stove for him." She pulls a large pot out of the fridge and turns the stove on.

"I don't hear any talking in the bedroom, but I need to get

into the bathroom to take a piss after all that beer. You think they'll notice if I sneak through the bedroom?"

Juni laughs at me and answers, "You're too big to sneak anywhere. Just knock and go do your thing. I need to go too, so they can't hog the facilities."

"Okay, well, c'mon then. There's power in numbers." I take her hand and we approach the bedroom door. We listen for a moment and hear low voices. I knock politely and announce, "Jack! We need to use the bathroom, and we're coming in." Simultaneously I open the door, and our jaws drop.

Thirteen

JUNIPER

"NICE ONE, JACK," I SAY IN A NASTY TONE. I WAS PREPARED to confront Blakelee, but this is too much of a shock to ignore.

Jack is standing next to the bed with his arms wrapped securely around his ex, looking like he never wants to let her go. My heart sinks. It's hard to breathe, and I feel sick. So sick, in fact, I don't wait for his answer. I run ahead of Asher and slam the bathroom door behind me. I'm so afraid all of my beer and snacks are about to make a second appearance I turn on the cold tap and splash my face over and over. The icy water refreshes me, so I dry myself off. I then take care of business so I can turn the bathroom over to Asher.

Opening the door again, I see Asher with his back to Jack

and Blakelee waiting at the door. His arms are crossed, and his face is devoid of all joy. He shoves past me into the bathroom as I slide past him. He's one unhappy dude, that's for sure.

"Care to explain?" I ask—because I'm nosy. And angry.

Blakelee speaks up in a snotty tone and announces, "Well, obviously, as you can see, he still loves me!"

Jack's expression is sad and resolved. He looks like he needs to clear his head, and by the time he's ready to speak, Asher is back in the room with us—glowering. I can't tell anything from Blakelee's expression because she won't look me in the eye, and that makes me feel even worse.

"I've been trying to explain to Blakelee that she needs to leave," he finally tells us, and I can suddenly breathe again. "But she's been determined to stick around and show me how much she still loves me."

"I do love you, Jack!" Blakelee whines. "I can't leave you. And it's obvious you still have feelings for me."

"Fine," Asher says with a wicked grin. This expression is scarier than his glower.

Jack and Blakelee's heads snap to attention as they stare at Asher.

"We could even the odds if Blakelee stays." He says with a gleam in his eyes. "Juni and I agree she's a beautiful woman, and maybe she's a bit immature, but we could get her to grow up—right, Juni?"

"Oh, yeah. She'd feel like a *real* woman around us, and we could show her a good time," I purr. "Besides, I don't know if the two of you have looked outside, but it's a frozen mess out there. You'd probably kill yourself just trying to navigate the stairs. So you might as well spend the night, Blakelee. With all of us. We can show you what it's like to have multiple partners all at once. You might even be able to have two dicks in you simultaneously. It's amazing."

Blakelee's mouth drops open, and it's not a good look for her. She stares at Jack as if asking for an explanation. He looks at Asher and me like we've sprouted two heads. I sidle up to Jack and wrap my arm around him, asking, "Do you want to make Blakelee part of us?" I stroke her arm as I gaze at Jack. That sweater of hers feels good. I wonder idly where she got it.

Jack's eyes almost pop out at me.

Asher approaches Blakelee and fiddles with a lock of her hair. "You're so pretty," he whispers. "I'd love to fuck that juicy peach of yours." He lowers his gaze to indicate her butt. "Mmm. Juni would be so good at going down on you too. She has experience with women."

Blakelee squirms out of Jack's embrace and away from Asher. "What is wrong with you people?" she cries. "I thought you were all in a committed relationship!"

"One that you seem all too anxious to break up," I tell her. "We're just trying to keep Jack, and if keeping him means adding you, that's what we'll do."

Just then there is a booming crack of thunder, and the sound of hail hitting the roof is deafening. It only lasts a few seconds, and then another thunderbolt rumbles from farther away. At least it's receding, and now it seems to be raining. Well, that's an improvement.

"I don't want to join a bunch of *freaks*," Blakelee almost shrieks.

Asher and I grin as Jack gets a knowing expression on his face. "Sorry, Blakelee. Asher, Juni, and I are a fixed deal. If you want me, you get all three of us. As I said before, it's time for you to go—unless you want to be part of our ménage." With a mock-sad expression he adds, "I would love to get off while watching Juni and Asher pleasure you. You have no idea how arousing that is."

"I'll gladly leave you freaks!" She pivots away and stomps out of the room. In the main living area, she starts struggling to yank on her boots. She left her coat in the bathroom, though, so I doubt she'll be leaving anytime soon.

Jack wraps his arms tightly around both of us and says in a serious voice, "What you saw was me trying to prevent her from slapping me. She'd just announced she hated me and took a swing. That's why I had her all wrapped in an embrace. She goes from loving to hating back and forth like a metronome. I thought I had her convinced to go back to Lexington, but when she heard the two of you needed to come in, it was like she wanted to fight about it all over again and save face or something. The fact is, she is obviously a gold digger, and her mother has encouraged it. That woman didn't give a crap about me until she read the article in *Kentucky's*

Best. But as soon as the magazine hit the stands, I'm suddenly more than good enough for her precious daughter—bisexual or not. This whole business of 'needing' me is financial—she let it slip that she doesn't have a job and hopes to be supported. Those stars in her eyes when she looks at me see dollar signs, not me. Now that I don't want her, I think she hates my guts."

"I'm sorry, Jack. It has to hurt to realize how she truly feels," I tell him as I hug him. He feels so good in my arms.

"Eh, not really. I got over the hurt a long time ago. Now I feel justified in telling her to hit the road. Speaking of roads, what was you said about the driving conditions?"

"It was starting to ice up pretty badly, and now the streets are deserted. I guess people got the message and went home," I tell him.

Jack's phone buzzes in his pocket, and when he retrieves it, he says, "It's a message from my gallery manager who said she sent people home as soon as it started to look treacherous outside and locked up the gallery." He looks at us. "We can't exactly send Blakelee out in this to drive back to Lexington. I'm going to call the inn and see if they have a room for the night."

We all wander out into the living room and find Blakelee still wrestling with her boots and crying angrily, "Now I have stupid mud all over my nice clothes!" She's acting like a petulant four-year-old, but I'm not surprised.

Jack makes his call, and we hear him say, "Thanks, Betty.

We'll bring her over right away. You said dinner and breakfast are included? Great. Charge one night to my credit card if you would, please. If she wants to stay longer, that's up to her." He rattles off the number, thanks the innkeeper again, and disconnects. "I guess there was a last-minute cancellation, so that's good news." He regards Blakelee and says, "Go get your coat. Asher and I are going to see that you make it safely down the stairs and over to the Honeybee Hollow Inn. It's a nice place, and as you heard, your room and board are paid for tonight. They have a terrific restaurant."

Blakelee sniffles and gives him a pleading look. "Will you at least have dinner with me?"

Jack returns her pathetic plea with a bland expression. "Sorry, Blakelee. I have plans with Juni and Asher. You'll have to figure out how to cut your own food."

She huffs at him as she flounces away, stomping more mud through the house to retrieve her coat, and we hear water running. When she returns, her face has fewer mascara streaks on it. It's a much better look. The men grab their hats, coats, and gloves and open the door.

Asher smiles and exclaims, "If you don't like the weather in Kentucky, wait five minutes and it'll change! Look at that." The ice has already melted off the steps, so he grabs her suitcase while Jack takes Blakelee by the arm and propels her out the door behind Asher.

Such gentlemen, I think to myself. *I love them so much.* I go and get the mop to clean up again before they get back.

♡♡♡

When they do get back, they're so relieved and content, I ask, "Are you both hungry for spaghetti yet? The sauce is hot, and I can boil the pasta while you get out of your coats."

Asher grins and says, "As long as we're taking off our coats, why don't we keep going and get rid of everything? I'm not hungry enough for dinner yet, but I'd sure like to taste a few other goodies."

"A man with a great idea," Jack agrees. "Let's turn the sauce down and head to the bedroom."

So we all shuck our clothes and tumble into Jack's big bed. We grope, kiss, fondle, and stroke everything that's available. And there is so much glorious naked skin on display, I can hardly contain myself. At one point, I have dicks in both hands while Asher and Jack kiss each other deeply. I scoot down and trade back and forth licking and sucking them, and I stroke the two of them, pressing their erections together. They are so wonderful this way. I'm hungry for my men, so I ask, "Can you guys DP me? I'm feeling empty and need you both to fill me up the way only you can do."

With a big grin, Jack disengages and pulls a bottle of lube from his nightstand. We all dispensed with condoms quite a while ago, and the enjoyment I get from this still feels like a miracle. I love the intimate contact and even the messiness of all the cum from two men at once.

"On your knees, ass up," Asher orders, and I quickly comply. I crave this part as much as I love their dicks in me. With two men kissing and playing with my body, I can't help squirming and moaning. Carefully, Asher penetrates my backside with his fingers, stretching me to accommodate his dick. Together, they probe me—Asher in back and Jack in my pussy, encouraging me with words of love. Jack finger-fucks me with one hand and stokes my clit perfectly with the other. I ought to feel vulnerable in this position, but I feel nothing but tenderness from these two precious men. I am completely cared for by them this way.

Satisfied that I'm stretched enough, Asher shifts position to lie on the bed. I'm still butt-high, so I swallow his dick and let Jack bring me closer and closer to an orgasm with his clever hands. When I'm nearly there, I tell him, "Okay, I'm ready to move." I flip over with my back to Asher and sink my bottom over him, taking his entire shaft into my hole. I love the burn I get each time we do this, and I shiver as he gasps. Pleasure floods my body.

Jack smiles at us lovingly as I settle onto Asher. He then bends down and sucks my clit into his mouth, knowing exactly what that does to me. With a long moan, I come, reaching for Jack's shoulders.

"Yes!" I cry. "It's so good. I need you too now, Jack, please."

Asher pulls me down to his chest and finds my terribly sensitive clit. As Jack enters me, Asher continues to manipulate me to wring more spasms of pleasure out of me. It's simply perfection—in fact, almost too much. Asher groans as I jerk and twitch with untold gratification.

"Ahh," he moans, "There you both are. I feel you, Jack. Fuck us. Oh, you both feel *so* good."

As Jack picks up speed and begins to slide in and out, I shake with yet another orgasm. I feel them rubbing together inside me, and the sensation never fails to make me crazy. I clamp them with my muscles and hear Asher grunt and laugh. I wish I could see his face, but I content myself with looking at the love reflected in Jack's beautiful eyes. Even though it's rather chilly in the bedroom, soon we're all coated with a sheen of sweat.

Jack pounds in and out, in and out, and I clamp and release my muscles in time with him. Asher begins to swear over and over in whispered benedictions. Jack shoves in and out and finally hangs his head and shakes. "Thank you!" he cries.

Asher is the last to come, and he does so with a bellow and then laughs. "This is the most fun I've ever had in my life!" he cries.

And that makes Jack and me laugh, too, because each time we do this, he says that. "Even better than last time?" I ask.

"Even better," he assures us. "The best ever."

Oh, how I love these men.

Fourteen

THE REST OF THE WINTER IS FAIRLY MILD. WE HAVE A FEW flurries here and there, but not enough to close businesses or disrupt lives.

Halden Dahl's crew comes and removes the couple of unsold pieces he had left in the gallery, and we ship the sold ones to their respective homes. Halden happily agrees to do another exhibit with us in two years. We change out the gallery to a painting and sculpture exhibit for another well-known Louisville artist, David E. Bernard. I have a great feeling about this show because this man's work is as amazing as Halden's.

When I decided to open a gallery, I thought I could do it well, but I had no expectations it would be this much of a success. It's quite a thrill, and I love that I've made a good living independent from my family's money. I must admit having a generous inheritance from my grandparents has been a huge boost. Truth be told, I could live on it luxuriously for the rest of my life and never work another day. But knowing that I can make a success of myself? Priceless.

I haven't heard another peep from Blakelee, but I did hear from a friend in Lexington that the reason Blakelee ghosted me in the first place was that her mother went around telling everyone I'd sold my house and moved away because I was having financial difficulties. She couldn't fathom that I just fell in love with a small town and wanted a change. But when the article came out and mentioned my family's vast wealth, her mom reconsidered and sent Blakelee down here to see me —knowing full well that I'm an only child and the heir to their fortune. Now apparently Blakelee is back on the hunt for a sugar daddy, and her mother is pissed at her for messing things up with me. I'm glad to be removed from her life, and I have to hand it to Juni and Asher for helping to expose her true feelings. "Freaks"—that's what she called us. Well, that stings a bit, but I refuse to let it bother me. I have two amazing people to share my life with now, and today I'm going to surprise them.

The fact is, we all have our own places to live, and the

properties are each well-suited to one person, but I'm ready for more permanence with them, so tonight I plan to talk to them about my idea.

Over a candlelit dinner (that I had catered by the Honeybee Hollow Inn), I ask, "So, Juni, have you ever considered renting out the apartment over Hot Stuff to make some extra money? Housing in town is really at a premium right now, and you could make a tidy profit from it."

She eyes me and then glances at Asher and asks, "Where do you propose I live if I do that?"

"I'll get to that," I say with a smile and look at Asher. "Is it crucial for you to live right in the middle of your camp? Could you maybe live… oh… next door possibly?"

Asher grins at me, catching on quickly. "Next door would be fine."

I breathe a sigh of relief and announce, "That's wonderful because I just bought the five acres next to the camp on the opposite shore of Paradise Pond, and I have an appointment with an architect tomorrow to go over building plans for a house. But I'll only build it if you'll both move in with me. You'll have as much or as little input on the plans as you wish. But I want us to have our own place together and live together formally. What do you say?"

"Can Asher design us a cool bathroom?"

We both laugh at Juni's request. "Of course," I say. "He can design as much as he wants, but he won't have to do the heavy lifting this time… or clean it himself. I'll hire us a household staff."

"Can we get a dog?" she asks.

"As many as you like."

"Then it's settled," Asher says, "We're building our dream house and moving in together like a real family—dogs and all."

"Yes, we are," she says with a huge smile.

"My heart is so full right now," I tell them and can't wait to call Weston and tell him how well this has turned out for all of us. "I'm so happy. I love you both forever."

"Same here," says Juni, choking up.

"Forever," Asher agrees. "We need to celebrate."

So we leave our dishes where they are and head to the bedroom.

Let the celebration begin.

The End

IF YOU'D LIKE TO READ WESTON ALISTER'S STORY, PLEASE check out Group Hug for more MMF fun!

Madison Lassiter and Halden Dahl's story is told in Savor This.

Read Tanner Lassiter's story in The Rule of 3, also an MMF book.

Find out more about Dolly Gunn's books in Save Her.

The next book in the Honeybee Hollow series is Buddy System

Coming May 15, 2025 in the Honeybee Hollow series: Everybody Knows

Https://www.ariellatalix.com

Acknowledgments

Had it not been for an assignment from the Kentuckiana Romance Writers to write a small-town Kentucky short story or novella for an anthology, this novella likely never would have happened. But I love my Honeybee Hollow so much, it was an easy choice to delve more into the local residents. It's as if the town itself is a character in the books that follow. This story was first published in Double Down on Love, but I now own the copyright for my contribution. I encourage you to purchase the anthology because all sales go straight to pancreatic cancer research. Please consider the book.

It's been a while since I wrote *Jack of Hearts*, but I still need to acknowledge my wonderful team. Dar Albert, my amazing cover artist, Amy Maranville- my talented editor, Mattie Davenport- my terrific proofreader, and my always available and helpful beta reader Susan. I would be lost without them and their fabulous talents.

But mostly I need to thank my loyal readers all over the world who continue to read and enjoy my stories. You are why

I do this. I wish I could meet each of you personally and express my gratitude.

Ariella Talix

ariella@ariellatalix.com

Every book is a standalone story with no cliffhanger.

Each series is more fun when read in order, however. Often characters show up again because I can't help myself.

Contemporary Romance

The Drummonds:

Porter the Importer

Make Believe

The Artist

Lovers in Louisville (Spin-off from The Drummonds):

Save Her

Saving Him

Savor This

Contemporary MMF Romance

The Perfect Number (Spin-off from Savor This):

The Rule of 3

The Passion of 3

Living the Fantasy:

Just Curious

Compelling Urges

Standalone:

Group Hug

Honeybee Hollow Series:

Jack of Hearts (MMF spin-off from Group Hug)

Buddy System (MMF spin-off from *Jack of Hearts*)

Everybody Knows (MF romance) May 15, 2025

Historical MMF Romance

Hearts of Gold:

The Golden Rush

Fiddle and Fire

Casting Vows

Anthologies

Double Down on Love (*Jack of Hearts*) with the Kentuckiana
Romance Writers

The Drummonds

Lovers in Louisville

The Perfect Number

Living the Fantasy